West Along
the Wagon Road

1852

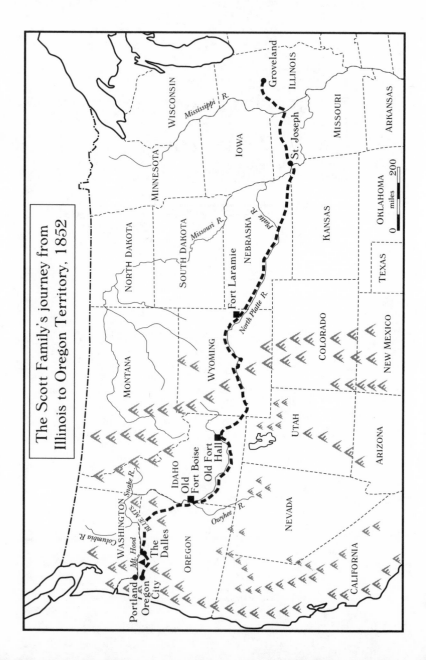

The Scott Family's journey from Illinois to Oregon Territory, 1852

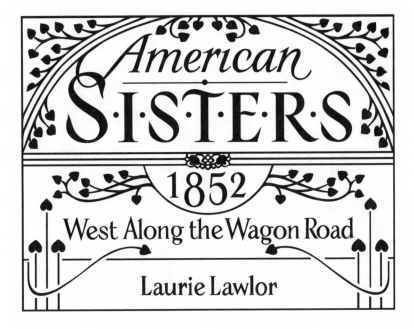

American
S·I·S·T·E·R·S

1852
West Along the Wagon Road

Laurie Lawlor

A MINSTREL® HARDCOVER
PUBLISHED BY POCKET BOOKS

New York   London   Toronto   Sydney   Tokyo   Singapore

Special thanks to Frances Duniway and the David Duniway heirs for providing permission for use of excerpts on pages 1–2 from *Crossing Over the Great Plains by Ox-Wagons* by Harriet Scott Palmer and from *Journal of a Trip to Oregon* by Abigail Jane Scott on pages 28, 71, 72, 86, 135, 146, 152, 154.

A MINSTREL HARDCOVER

A Minstrel Book published by
POCKET BOOKS, a division of Simon & Schuster Inc.
1230 Avenue of the Americas, New York, NY 10020

ISBN: 0-671-01551-6

First Minstrel Books hardcover printing September 1998

10 9 8 7 6 5 4 3 2 1

A MINSTREL BOOK and colophon are registered trademarks of Simon & Schuster Inc.

Cover design by Gina DiMarco
Cover illustration by Dorothea Sharp/Christie's Images

Printed in the U.S.A.

For my teacher
Kay Keefe

Books by Laurie Lawlor

The Worm Club
How to Survive the Third Grade
Addie Across the Prairie
Addie's Long Summer
Addie's Dakota Winter
George on His Own
Gold in the Hills

Heartland series
Heartland: Come Away with Me
Heartland: Take to the Sky
Heartland: Luck Follows Me

American Sisters series
West Along the Wagon Road 1852

Chapter

1

. . . *The spring of 1852 ushered in so many prepara-*
tions, great work of all kinds. I remember relations
coming to help sew; tearful partings; little gifts of re-
membrance exchanged; the sale of the farm, the buying
and breaking of unruly oxen; the loud voices of the
men; and the general confusion. The first of April
came. We were on our way to Oregon Territory. The
long line of covered wagons, so clean and white . . .
the loud callings and hilarity: many came to see us
off. We took a last view of our dear Illinois homestead
as it faded from sight. . . .

An open country was now before us. The melting
snows had made the streams high; the roads nearly
impassable. . . . When we reached Wyoming, this side

of Fort Laramie, the passing of dear beloved Mother was a crushing blow to all our hopes. We had to journey on and leave her in a lonely grave—a feather-bed as a coffin and the grave protected from the wolves by stones heaped upon it. The rolling hills were ablaze with beautiful wild roses—it was the twentieth of June, and we covered Mother's grave with the lovely roses, so the cruel stones were hid from view. We named the spot Castle Hill.

—Duck

Duck ran as fast as she could toward the granite outcropping that looked like a great, gray giant slumbering in the middle of the open plain. She lifted the ragged edge of her long skirt and tucked it inside her belt so that she could leap over bunches of prickly pear. She darted around clumps of sage.

Faster! Faster! As she pumped her skinny legs and dug her heels into the dry, brittle ground, she forgot everything that had happened, everything she left behind. At that moment she was aware only of the rush and blur of her own movement. The sun beat down on the top of her head. Her brown hair blew every which way in the hot wind. Sweat trickled down her forehead into her brown eyes. Her throat ached, but she did not pause to rest or catch her breath.

"Duck!" commanded nineteen-year-old Fanny. "Stop!"

"Wait for us!" pleaded Jenny, seventeen.

Fifteen-year-old Maggie, who straggled farthest behind, called, "I can't keep—" The rest of her words were lost in the howling breeze.

Duck paid no attention to her three oldest sisters—she kept running. She was eleven years old, the youngest of the four girls, and was determined to reach Independence Rock first. She'd climb to the top and use the jackknife she had borrowed to carve a message in big letters for all the world to see.

D. SCOTT FROM ILLINOIS—JUNE 29, 1852

Then wouldn't Father and her five sisters and three brothers be impressed?

At last she reached the rock's shadow. Its dark coolness swallowed her. Straight ahead, rising three hundred feet or more—higher than the tallest church spire back home—stood the rock. The rough surface of its enormous wall was scrawled with names and dates scratched and carved and painted in red and black letters. "Independence," "Wm. Sublette," "Moses Harris," "1841" and hundreds more messages from people she did not know—all going west just as she and her family were.

Duck reached out. Closer, closer. *There!* She slapped her palm against the rock. The sting made her accomplishment feel real. She was first!

She turned and slumped against the rock. She gulped for air. Her knees shook, but she had made it. She smiled and watched her sisters struggling in the distance. How ridiculous they looked! They ran toward the rock in mincing, ladylike steps. Their skirts flapped about their ankles. Their sunbonnets heaved left and right on their heads like ships' sails on a stormy sea.

First came Jenny. She was the most determined of the three. Nicknamed String Bean by their brothers, Jenny was skinny with long legs. She had mischievous blue eyes and dull brown hair.

Next came Fanny. She was tall, just like Father, and had the same fierce, dark-eyed stare. Her brown hair was parted severely in the middle. Her small, pinched mouth rarely smiled at Duck.

Earlier that afternoon Fanny had clearly not been pleased when she noticed Duck trailing her and Jenny and Maggie as they left the wagon train and headed on foot for Independence Rock. "Nobody asked you to come along," Fanny grumbled. "Aren't you supposed to be helping herd cattle?"

"Father said, 'A few can go if you get back before we ford the river,'" Duck insisted. "He didn't say *which* few he meant."

"What harm is there in Duck joining us?" Maggie asked. "It isn't every day that you get a chance to visit something so famous and grand as Independence Rock."

Good old Maggie.

"All right," Fanny growled. "But try for once to stay out of trouble."

Now Duck watched Fanny stumbling through the sage and found the sight very satisfying. *I stayed out of trouble and I beat you here.* Duck cupped her hands around her mouth. "Slowpokes!" she hollered.

Fanny refused to look at Duck. Instead, she turned and shouted at Maggie, the very last. "Come on!"

Maggie did not reply. Her arms moved back

and forth, as if she were trying her best to catch up. She was the frailest and the prettiest of Duck's three oldest sisters. She had the same brown hair as the others. What was different were her lovely smile and large blue eyes that often seemed very amused or very surprised.

As Maggie ran, something kept sticking to her skirt. Was it prickers? Every so often, she stopped, unhooked the material, and keep trotting. This time she wiped her face with her sleeve, sped a few more feet, stumbled forward, and vanished.

"Maggie!" Duck shouted. When her sister did not reappear and it seemed clear that neither Jenny nor Fanny was going back to help Maggie, Duck left the base of Independence Rock. She ran past her other two sisters to the spot where she had seen Maggie drop from sight. What if she was hurt? "Maggie," she called. "Where are you?"

No answer.

"Maggie!"

"I'm over here!" Maggie cried.

Duck followed the sound of her sister's voice beyond a fragrant clump of sun-drenched sage. She looked down. There was Maggie, crumpled in a heap in a shallow hole, laughing. "What are you doing down there?" Duck demanded. "Is your leg broke?"

"I'm perfectly fine. Help me out," Maggie said. "I didn't plan on paying any calls on prairie dogs today."

Duck giggled. She extended her hand to her sister and pulled with all her might. Maggie scrambled out of the hole and brushed dirt from her skirt. "That was very kind of you to rescue me. But do you know you look very unladylike?"

Duck looked down at her skirt, which was still tucked inside her belt so that her worn, patched breeches were plain as day. "Oh, well," she said and shrugged. "If Father would let me, I'd wear overalls like Sonny and Harvey. A dress makes no sense when you have to ride a horse all day."

"Don't be silly. Girls don't wear overalls." Maggie leaned over and adjusted Duck's skirt. She tied Duck's sunbonnet in a proper bow under her chin. "When are you going to start acting civilized?"

Duck sighed and didn't answer. She didn't enjoy it when Maggie pretended to be her mother. All fussy and bossy. She liked Maggie better when she was her friend, the person who listened to her secrets and dreams and jokes. The one who told her scary stories and helped her fly kites decorated with fierce dragon faces. "Come on," Duck said. She took Maggie's hand and began walking. "Uncle Levi let me borrow his knife. We can climb up and carve our names on Independence Rock. Someday someone will—" She shielded her eyes and looked up at the very top of Independence Rock.

"What's the matter?" Maggie asked.

"Is that Jenny and Fanny up there?"

"Slowpokes!" two figures taunted. "We're first! We're first!"

Duck scowled. Fanny and Jenny were cheats. She had been first, not them, and they knew it. They had purposefully not gone back to help Maggie so that they could scramble to the top before Duck. Why did her oldest sisters always manage to get their own way? It wasn't fair.

"Hello, Jenny! Hello, Fanny!" Maggie called and waved good-naturedly. "How did you get up there?"

"It's our little secret," Jenny said. She laughed and disappeared.

"Independence Rock is much taller than I imagined," Maggie said. "I don't know if I can climb that high."

"If those two made it, there must be a way," Duck replied. "Come on. Let's look around on the other side."

She and Maggie followed the base of the rock and found a well-worn path that led up along a broken ridge of boulders. "We'll climb up here. It's as easy as walking up the courthouse steps back home." She scrambled nimbly atop the first rock.

"I don't know. It doesn't look safe," Maggie said. "What if the wobbly slabs come loose? What if the whole thing tumbles apart? We'll be buried alive."

"Don't be such a coward," Duck said. She kept climbing higher and higher. She stopped every so often to show Maggie a secure place to step. "Look over there, Maggie." She pointed east, the way they'd come. "Do you see that purplish ridge? I bet that's Castle Hill."

"Maybe," Maggie replied and blinked hard. "And what's that?"

In the distance Duck could see a cloud of dust churned up by hundreds of wagons, some moving six abreast. "More travelers," Duck said. Together, the girls watched the approaching oxen and wagons that seemed as small as a trudging army of ants.

Duck shifted her gaze west toward the pale, shimmering plains. Overhead, shiplike clouds passed, casting enormous shadows on the ground below. It seemed to her as if the whole world around Independence Rock had become a circle of sky. The outer edges, where the sky touched the ground, seemed to bend and waver—always just out of sight, out of reach. Somewhere farther west beyond these endless plains she had heard that there were mountains so high, the snow never melted. There were deserts so wide, it took days to cross.

"More than a thousand miles. Father said that's how far we still have to go before we reach Oregon," Duck said. "That's a very long way, isn't it?"

Maggie nodded. "You must be brave, Duck."

Duck bit her lip. *A thousand miles. How will we make it without Mother?* "Do you miss Mother terribly, too?"

"Of course," Maggie said slowly. "Sometimes

I wake up in the middle of the night and pretend nothing's different. Nothing's changed."

"Does that make you feel any better?" Duck asked hopefully.

"No," Maggie admitted.

Duck frowned. "Do you think we'll ever be able to find her grave again?"

"Castle Hill is a beautiful spot," Maggie said. "Remember how the view from up there overlooks the ravine? We'll never forget where Castle Hill is. Never."

Duck did not feel so certain. All along the trail to Oregon she and her sisters and brothers had counted fresh-made graves—sometimes five or six a day. All victims of the dreaded cholera. Most had no markers. Others were simple scrawled boards that said: OUR ONLY CHILD. LITTLE MARY or BELOVED. 1852. The shallowest ones were dug up by animals. Sometimes skulls, bones, grave clothes, and old shoes lay scattered beside the wagon ruts. What had once been a curiosity now filled her with a new kind of terror. What if the same thing happened to their mother's grave? What if it were lost forever?

"Don't look so sad, Duck. Everything will be

fine," Maggie said. "You'll see." She reached out and briefly rested one finger beneath Duck's upturned chin—the same way Mother would have done. She smiled at Duck, but Duck knew her sister too well. Maggie felt just as scared and worried as she did.

Chapter 2

When Duck and Maggie finally reached the broad, flat top of Independence Rock, they discovered their two sisters standing beside a scrawny young man who held a bucket in one hand. Nearby grew a small, bent juniper and a few hardy tufts of grass that had managed to survive between cracked boulders.

"Hello," called Jenny. "Too bad you didn't get here sooner. This nice gentleman from Columbus, Ohio, had just enough pine tar and hog fat left to write our names. See?" She pointed to the black letters painted at their feet:

JENNY AND FANNY S

The skinny, squinting young man seemed to brighten considerably when he noticed Maggie. Bashfully he showed her the empty bucket. "All g-g-gone," he stammered. "Sorry."

Maggie smiled.

"If my slow-as-molasses sisters had arrived sooner," Jenny announced, "I'm sure you would have included their names, too."

Duck frowned. She wished she could push her boastful sister off the edge.

"I must be going," the young man said. He tried to tip his hat toward Maggie but dropped it on the ground. He turned bright red, bent over to pick it up and dropped it again.

"Farewell!" Fanny primly waved her handkerchief.

Jenny muffled a giggle. "Safe trip!" she called.

The young man's glance never once left Maggie. Duck watched in bewilderment as the scrawny fellow tried to walk backward so that he would not have to look away from her sister. He tripped, regained his balance, fumbled with the bucket, put his hat on his head, and began climbing down the rock.

"If I didn't know better, I'd say that poor clumsy fellow's sweet on Maggie," Jenny said.

"Aren't they all?" Fanny replied, shooting Maggie one of her sourest glances.

Maggie blushed but refused to speak.

Duck didn't know what to make of their encounter. At first she wondered if the hog-fat fumes in his bucket had made the man from Ohio so giddy and stupid. But it wasn't the first time she had seen a young man turn idiotic when he met Maggie. Her sister never said anything fascinating. She never did anything particularly remarkable. She just smiled. Why was that enough to make young men lose their senses?

Duck rolled her eyes in disgust. She was glad the scrawny fellow was gone. His presence had made her two other sisters meaner than usual. When that happened, Duck knew to watch out. Sooner or later their meanness had a way of finding a target—often Duck herself. To become as invisible as possible, Duck crouched on the ground beside a rock with no writing on it.

She slipped Uncle Levi's knife from her pocket and began carving a large *D* into the soft, crumbling surface. *Duck* was her nickname, given to her by Grandfather. When she was two years old, she chased and cuddled the ducklings in Grandfather's barnyard so determinedly, he called her Duck. The name stuck. Nobody in the family ever used her real name, Harriet Louise. Next she carved S-C-O-T-T. Somehow the letters didn't come out as clearly as she'd hoped. If only she had her own bucket of gunpowder, tar, and buffalo grease, then she'd do a proper job.

Jenny, Fanny, and Maggie sat down on a nearby boulder to rest. For the time being they seemed to have forgotten about Duck's presence. "Fanny," Jenny said with a dramatic sweep of her hand toward the distant plains, "wouldn't you say it's difficult to imagine a more sublime scene?"

Fanny nodded wearily.

"Independence Rock is a most singular place. I intend to write about everything we've seen today in the journal when we get back," Jenny said.

"If you ask me, this rock looks like a big bread bowl turned upside down," Fanny said. She slipped off her worn shoes and rubbed her feet.

"Excellent. I'll remember your words exactly for the journal. What would you say, Maggie? What does this rock remind you of?"

Maggie was silent for a few moments. "I'm not as poetical as you. I'd say it looks like an enormous egg."

"And you, Duck?" Jenny asked, turning to her sister. "What do you think?"

"I'd say a large monster — something cheating and boastful with brown hair and blue eyes whose name starts with a *J*," Duck replied sweetly.

Jenny jumped to her feet, her hands curled into fists. "Why you little . . ."

Duck shielded her head with her arms.

"That's enough!" Maggie said quickly. "You know what Father will do if he finds out there's been fighting."

Reluctantly Jenny sat down again. She reclined on the flat rock, her arms crossed in front of herself. When none of her sisters were watching, Duck stuck her tongue out at Jenny.

"Aren't those clouds turning stormy?" Fanny announced.

"Which ones?" Jenny demanded. She sat up, peering in the distance.

"Those," Fanny said, pointing toward a growing, bruise-colored thunderhead to the northwest. "I think we'd better go back."

Abruptly the sun vanished. Cold wind gusted across the rock. Dust flew. "Was that lightning?" Maggie asked nervously.

"Where?" Jenny asked.

"There!" Duck said. She pointed. A small, slender finger of lightning illuminated the darkened sky. Thunder rumbled. Duck quickly closed the jackknife and hid it in her pocket.

The three oldest girls stood up and ran toward the edge. They peered down. "The wagons!" Maggie said and gasped. "Father's starting to ford. They're leaving us behind."

"We've been abandoned!" Jenny cried.

Fanny wailed. "We'll be struck by lightning and no one will ever find our poor, charred bodies up here!"

"Stop blubbering and put on your shoes, Fanny," Jenny said. "We've got to get off this rock. Run for your lives!"

Duck and her sisters climbed down the rock as the wind blew harder. Rain mixed with hail pelted the side of the rock and stung their skin. Their clothes were quickly soaked through. Duck slipped on a slick rock. She regained her balance. Slowly she descended and could finally jump to the ground. "Come on, Maggie!" she called. "You're almost to the bottom now."

Maggie's teeth were chattering. She looked pale. Duck grabbed her hand and together the two girls raced with Fanny and Jenny back to the Sweetwater River. They cowered low to the ground and covered their ears with their hands whenever lightning suddenly illuminated the sky. The ground shook with thunder. Duck could feel the rumble up through the soles of her feet.

When the girls reached the water's edge, the hail and rain stopped. Oxen bellowed. The last of the five wagons was in the river and had nearly reached midstream. After two months on the trail, the once brilliant white wagon canvas top was now tattered and dirty. The wagon's green and yellow paint, once so hopeful and bright, was now mud-spattered and chipped.

"Wait for us!" Duck shouted.

Duck's thirteen-year-old sister, Kit, poked her head out of the back of the last wagon. She was safe and dry and smiled triumphantly. "Father can't hear you," Kit called. "He's already on the other side. He said leaving you four behind would teach you a lesson."

Duck scowled at Kit, who was just two years older and barely an inch taller. Why did Kit always try to act as if she knew everything? Like Duck's other sisters, Kit had the same straight brown hair. Although her eyes were blue, she and Duck were often mistaken for twins by strangers.

"Father was going to leave us to ford on our own?" Duck demanded with disbelief. *How can he be so cruel?*

"Hello, Duck!" Chat called. Her dark curly head popped up beside Kit in the opening at the back of the wagon. She was a pudgy five-year-old with big dark eyes and a wild imagination. Her real name was Katherine but everyone called her Chat because she talked and sang constantly. "Hurry up before the fishes eat you. The fishes are everywhere. They will nibble you. They will —"

"Sit down and be quiet for once," Kit commanded her pesky youngest sister. Chat disappeared from view. Kit turned to Duck and Maggie and shouted in a loud voice, "Father said, 'Let them wade across.' Those were his exact words. You're wet already, aren't you? The Sweetwater's only waist high. It's warmer than the Platte River."

Some of the hired men, who were already on the other side, one hundred feet away, began to hoot and holler. They bent over, doubled up with laughter and pointed at Duck and her wet, bedraggled sisters.

"Come on, gals. Swimming's not so bad! That's how the cows make it across, and they don't complain!" one of the hired men called.

Duck scowled and took Maggie's hand. "I would have liked the fun of wading well enough," she grumbled to her sister, "but I don't like to get joked about being left."

"Me neither," Maggie replied. "Do you think the fish will bite us?"

"Not if we keep moving fast enough," Duck said. She took a deep breath and trudged up to her knees. The swift current swirled around her legs, almost knocking her off balance. The soft sand of the river bottom nearly sucked off her shoes. How cold the water felt! Deeper, deeper yet.

"Keep walking," Maggie said.

Duck splashed a few more feet forward. Out of the corner of her eye, she spied Jenny and Fanny. They primly held the hems of their skirts out of the water, even though their dresses were as completely soaked as the pelts of drowned rats.

"Can you swim?" Maggie asked. Her teeth were chattering louder now and her lips were blue.

Duck shook her head.

"Me neither," Maggie replied.

When they reached the other side, Duck stumbled to dry land. She wrung out her skirt as best she could. That was when she noticed. Her pocket was empty. The knife had disappeared. "Uncle Levi's knife!" Duck said frantically to Maggie.

"We can't go back. There's no time," Maggie said. She pointed to the head of the wagons. In the distance they could both see Father's commanding figure atop his favorite mare. He was motioning with his arm and calling, "Chain up! Roll out!"

"What should I do?" Duck asked.

"Tell Uncle Levi what happened."

Duck groaned. "He'll be so angry. And what will Father do when he finds out I lost something I borrowed?"

Maggie shrugged. "Maybe Uncle Levi will let you pay him back."

"How? I haven't got any money." Miserably Duck stared at her muddy feet. She had to think. She had to come up with a plan.

"Here's Shuttleback, all saddled and waiting."

The unexpected voice made Duck jump. She looked up. There was John MacDonald, the twenty-year-old hired hand. He sat atop his horse while holding the reins of Duck's sorrel mare. His dusty brown hat was pulled down over his forehead so that Duck couldn't see his handsome dark eyes, but she knew he was smiling.

Suddenly Maggie let out a piercing, twittering giggle. The sound so surprised Duck, she rocked back on her heels. She stared at her sister with concern. "You gag on river mud or something?" Duck asked.

John chuckled.

"I'm perfectly fine," Maggie replied, blushing. She straightened her filthy apron and marched away.

"What's the matter?" Duck called, still perplexed.

"Leave me alone," Maggie replied coldly over her shoulder.

Duck watched her sister disappear inside one

of the wagons. She rubbed her forehead and frowned. *What did I do?* Duck took Shuttleback's reins from John. Back in Illinois he was the eldest son of the only Methodist minister in town. On the journey to Oregon he was simply another herder. "Any idea why Maggie's acting so strange?" Duck asked.

John shrugged and shook his head. "Women. Who can figure what they're thinking?" He gently kicked his horse and turned to ride to the front of the wagon train.

Duck watched him go. His words left a lonely, thorny feeling in the bottom of her stomach. Fanny and Jenny and Kit could be mysteriously moody and mean sometimes. Not Maggie. Not *her* Maggie. John had it all wrong. She turned and patted Shuttleback's dusty neck. "Maggie's not mad at me, is she, Shuttleback?"

The tall, homely sorrel mare snorted. She turned so that she could peer at Duck with her one good eye.

Duck smiled. "Don't bite me, Shuttleback," she said. "It's been a bad day. A very bad, wet day. I don't know what I'm going to tell Uncle Levi about his lost knife, do you?"

Shuttleback shook her head. Duck reached as

high as she could, grabbed the saddle horn, put one soggy foot in the stirrup, and swung her other soggy leg up on to the horse's broad sway back. High in the saddle, she hoped she looked dashing and brave, tall and free. A real cowboy who could race like the wind.

Duck gathered the reins and turned Shuttleback toward two oxen lazily nosing a few wisps of grass. "It's a good thing you're not children in my family," she called to the oxen. "No dawdling! Hard work never hurt anybody." Somehow the oxen were not impressed by Father's favorite phrase.

Father's belief in hard work was an important reason why the Scott family had come west. Oregon Territory offered free land, deep rich soil, leaping salmon, and mild, snowless winters. "A diligent man would be a fool to pass up an opportunity like this," Father had announced. Without asking Mother, he sold the farm in Illinois.

He planned their 3,000-mile trip carefully. A total of thirty-two oxen pulled the family's five heavy, springless wagons with strong canvas tops. The provision wagon was loaded with barrels and casks filled with hundreds of pounds of flour, hardtack, bacon, coffee, brown sugar, in addition to yeast, salt, and pepper for the three-month trip. The camp equipment wagon contained tents, extra bedding, tin plates, cups, and cooking utensils. The Salon Wagon, as it was named, served as a kind of parlor for Duck and her sisters. This wagon was used to haul clothing and bedding. Mother's Wagon, as it was called, served as the main riding place for the two youngest in the family: five-year-old Chat and three-year-old Wilkie. The fifth wagon was used to carry anything extra, mostly food items. Each wagon had a rifle hanging from a leather strap, its own tar bucket, and emergency equipment for repairs. Nine hired men took turns driving the wagons and herding the cattle.

Like the general of a small army, Father assigned Duck and each of her brothers and sisters jobs for the long journey. Fanny was head cook for everyone in the caravan. Jenny wrote every evening in the journal. Maggie helped with the journal or acted as cooking assistant. Sonny, nine, served as assistant wagon driver. Fourteen-year-old Harvey regularly drove one of the family's wagons. Kit kept an eye on the two youngest, Chat and Wilkie.

Duck's responsibility was to help Father's herders keep the family's three cows, ten extra oxen, two horses, and one pony from wandering off or scattering. On horseback she searched for strays, chased runaways, and tried to keep the cattle from drinking alkali-poisoned puddles. The cows were especially prone to run off into sloughs or become injured in thickets of prickly pear. Although she carried a lariat made of hemp, her only real power over the cattle was the sound of her voice and the ornery presence of Shuttleback. Shuttleback had a nasty temper and a nasty kick. The horses that bolted away during thunderstorms were more afraid of the big sorrel mare than of Duck. Nevertheless, she shouted and sang and soothed the cattle as best she could.

"Get moving!" Duck shouted to the oxen. The big beasts ambled single file between the wagon tracks. In the distance she heard the family's wagon wheels creak and groan. Every so often the air rang out with the loud *snap! snap! snap!* of the drivers' whips over the heads of the straining oxen. Deep in thought, she tried to imagine what she should say to Uncle Levi that evening when they stopped to make camp. How would she ever explain what had happened?

Chapter 3

We came 20 miles. The Sweetwater is clear and palatable. Immediately after leaving Independence Rock we came in sight of the well known Devil's Gate five miles ahead of us and when we came near enough we turned off the road about one mile and halted for the night opposite to it in a bend of the river.

Devil's Gate is indeed a sight worth seeing; the Sweetwater passes through it, and it really seems left by providence for the river to pass through as we can see no other place where it can find its way through the rocks. The cliffs of rock on either side are at least 400 feet in height and on the South Side almost perfectly perpendicular; We saw seven graves.

—*Maggie*

That evening the wagon drivers pulled the wagons into a half circle before unhitching the oxen to graze nearby. Unfortunately, there wasn't much grass, even though there were plenty of flowers—mostly blossoming wild pea and plum. Harvey and Sonny were sent out by Fanny to search for wood for the cooking fire but returned with only a few armfuls of sage roots chopped with an ax and dug up with their bare hands.

"Please don't complain about the grub," Fanny said when dinner was finally cooked. She handed Uncle Levi a tin plate of gristly salt pork and a small biscuit.

"Who's complaining, my dear?" Uncle Levi said jovially. He was a short, roly-poly man with a large stomach, helter-skelter eyebrows, and laughing eyes. "Your cooking is always delightful. It's the portions I mind. Perhaps John MacDonald will go off with his rifle and bring us fresh meat. That would make a great feast, wouldn't it, dearest Duck?"

Duck nodded. She took her plate and sat beside her uncle on the ground. She ate quickly, without really tasting anything. After months together on the trail, she had learned it was best to keep her mouth shut while Uncle Levi was eating. Dinner was his favorite time of the day, and he did not like to be disturbed. Conversation, he said, took away from his enjoyment of food.

"Delicious!" Uncle Levi said finally. He scraped his plate with his hand and licked his fingers with a loud smack. "With a pint of my favorite brew, this would be a fine meal. But of course I mustn't think of such things—am I right, dearest Duck?"

Duck smiled. They both knew Father's rule. Uncle Levi had been allowed on the trip only as long as he promised not to drink even one drop of liquor. So far he had managed to keep his word and stay sober. "Uncle Levi?" Duck asked, hoping to catch him in a good mood. "I have something to tell you. Something unfortunate."

"Not a terrible tragedy, I hope."

"Well, I suppose that would be how you look at it. Remember how I borrowed your jackknife?"

Uncle Levi nodded.

"You see, something happened while I was climbing Independence Rock."

"You weren't injured were you, dearest Duck?"

Miserably Duck shook her head. "I raced up to the rock so that I could be first. I wanted to beat my sisters and carve my name highest for everyone to see. Only nothing worked out the way I planned."

"You didn't make it to the top first?"

Duck shook her head.

"You didn't carve your name in huge letters visible for fifty miles?"

Duck shook her head again. To keep from looking at Uncle Levi, she twisted a dirty corner of her apron into a knot. "I lost your knife. I think it fell in the river when we tried to wade across. I couldn't go back to look for it because Father and everyone else were already mad at us for being late. I'm sorry, Uncle Levi." She tried to catch a quick glimpse of her uncle to see how angry he might be.

"I see," said Uncle Levi. He stroked his chin as if he were deep in thought.

He's going to tell Father. Now I'll really be in terrible trouble. Duck took a deep breath. "I'll pay you back, I promise. As soon as we get to Oregon, I'll find a job. I'll make some money and buy you a new knife. A bigger, better one.

I never meant to lose it. I was only trying to do something outstanding."

Uncle Levi leaned forward. A faint smile played across his lips. "Outstanding?"

Now that Duck could see that he wasn't angry with her, she felt relieved. She hunched forward and looked around to make sure no one else was listening. "Do you think," she said in a low voice, "that one day it might be possible that I will do something truly remarkable? Something famous?"

"It's possible, dearest Duck. Your father is remarkable. Your mother, bless her dear soul, was remarkable. You have several very accomplished, remarkable sisters and brothers equally talented. I would say that yes, someday you, too, will be remarkable."

"But how can you tell? I want to be sure."

Uncle Levi coughed. "Now turn a bit toward the fire light. That's right. Good. I can see from the shape of your head that you have some great adventures in store for you." He put his hand on the top of her head. He closed his eyes. When he removed his hand, he opened his eyes. "I used to be a phrenologist, you know. Made quite a penny back in Illinois reading people's fortunes by examining their skulls. You've got a remarkable skull. I can tell you that great adventures are in store for you."

"Great adventures?" Duck said. She thought about the disaster on Independence Rock and how she had been humiliated along the river when everyone laughed as she and her sisters had to wade across. "I don't think I'll ever have remarkable adventures or accomplish anything amazing," she said sadly. "I can't cook like Fanny. I can't write like Jenny. I'm not as pretty or kind as Maggie. I can't sing like Chat. As for Kit, well—"

"Well, what?"

"Well, I really don't want to be like her anyhow," Duck whispered. "I don't like her very much, you know."

"I've noticed," Uncle Levi said.

"I'm afraid," Duck said in a low voice, "I'm not a very remarkable person."

"Now, now!" Uncle Levi said. "Don't you know? Adventures await. To live fully you must seek them out and see them through doing what is right, no matter how hard."

Duck thought about what Uncle Levi said. It didn't make any sense. *Adventures await.* But where? She might be a shriveled old lady before she had a chance to do anything brave and amazing. Where were the adventures hiding? And how would she know when she found one? And what did *doing what is right, no matter how hard* mean? It all sounded so difficult and impossible. Duck only felt more confused than ever. She sighed with disappointment. Why did grown-ups always pretend to be helpful when they had no intention of being helpful at all?

"What's going on here?" Father demanded gruffly. He was a tall, ramrod-straight man with a hawklike nose. "Duck, aren't you supposed to be helping Fanny?"

"Good evening, Tucker," Uncle Levi said. His voice suddenly sounded high-pitched and strained. "We were just enjoying the evening. I was practicing a bit of phrenology—"

"Not that hogwash, Levi. That's nothing but a circus sideshow amusement." Father's voice boomed dangerously louder. His face became dangerously redder. He glared down at Uncle Levi. "I wouldn't be surprised if that Independence Rock escapade was partly your doing, too."

Uncle Levi shook his head and looked up at Father as innocently as a choirboy.

"Everyone must do their part on this journey," Father said. "We each have a responsibility. A destiny."

"That's exactly what I was telling Duck," Uncle Levi said.

Duck held her breath. *Here it comes. The lost jackknife.*

"Duck has adventures in store for her," Uncle Levi continued. "I'm sure of—"

Father's severe look was enough to silence Uncle Levi. Father took a deep breath and stared down at Duck. "You have a job to do. Not climbing up some misshapen pile of rocks without asking permission—"

"But, Father—" Duck protested.

"But nothing. You did not ask me. Do you know what might have happened during that storm while you were crawling around scribbling your names like all those other thousands of fools before you? The cattle might have run off. Lucky for us, John MacDonald had the sense to put two extra fellows on watch when the lightning started."

Duck hung her head. "I was just trying to do

something remarkable," she mumbled. "I didn't even get a chance to write out my name."

"I hope our leaving without you taught you a lesson. There is no room on this trip for silly sidetrips and ridiculous schemes. This wagon train has to run efficiently," Father said. Then he turned to Uncle Levi. "As for you, Levi, I forbid you to encourage irrational, foolhardy behavior. Do you understand?"

"Yes, Tucker," Uncle Levi replied timidly.

"Six daughters! Do you know what it is like to have six daughters?"

"No, Tucker."

"Do you know what will happen to the discipline, the routine around here if my six daughters start to think they're supposed to go off on adventures?"

"No, Tucker."

"Chaos. That's what. That is why there can be no more of these discussions," Father said. "Do I make myself clear?"

"Yes, Tucker."

"As for you, Duck," Father said, focusing his glare on his trembling daughter, "herding is *your* responsibility. You are to be vigilant watching the oxen, not searching for adventure. Do I make myself clear?"

Duck nodded slowly.

"You may report to Fanny," he continued. "She undoubtedly has something you can do to keep your mind off nonsense. Remember, hard work never hurt anybody." Father turned on his heel and walked away.

"Thank you," Duck whispered to Uncle Levi, "for not mentioning the knife to Father."

Uncle Levi stood up and made a stiff, gallant bow. "My dear, I am not concerned so much with lost jackknives as I am with lost dreams, lost hopes," he said and winked. "I know you'll replace that knife for me one day. In the meantime I want you to promise me something."

Duck bit her lip. "What?" she asked nervously.

"I want you to promise to live fully. To seek out adventures and see them through, doing what is right, no matter how hard."

"All right," Duck said halfheartedly. Deep down, she wondered if it would have been easier if Uncle Levi had simply become angry at her and told Father about the lost jackknife. Then she would have been punished and had it all over with then and there. *Doing what is right, no matter how hard.* How was she supposed to seek out adventures and see them through the way Uncle Levi said? She feared her promise would be impossible to keep.

Chapter

4

Duck walked across the camp and cautiously approached Fanny and Jenny near the provision wagon. By lantern light Fanny wiped the last of the tin plates and cups with a flour-sack rag. Jenny sat nearby on a barrel and stared at something in her lap.

Duck stood in the shadows. "Hello?" she called.

"Who's there?" Fanny replied.

"It's me. Duck."

"Oh, we thought it was someone important," Jenny replied. Her laughter sounded like a burbling swamp wren. The sound made Duck's stomach churn.

Fanny flourished the flour-sack rag. "You conveniently avoided clean-up again," she said, using her most imperial big-sister voice.

Duck decided to ignore Fanny's remark. "Father told me to see if you had anything else for me to do." She stepped into the light of the lantern.

Fanny looked critically at Duck. "You can take this bowl of soft bread and boiled milk to Wilkie," Fanny said. "I made it for him specially. Make sure he eats it."

Duck turned to leave when Fanny stopped her. "Why must you be so troublesome?" Fanny demanded. "The whole camp knows that Father is angry with you again. You weren't supposed to come with us today to Independence Rock. I warned you. But you stubbornly went along anyway. You wandered off and you didn't do your job. We each have a responsibility. What if one day I decided not to cook?"

Duck tried not to look incredulous. *Fanny purposefully disobey Father? Impossible.*

Fanny frowned. "Why do you vex poor Father so? He has a great deal on his mind right now."

Jenny licked the tip of her pencil and held it

poised above the journal page. "This might make another interesting episode in the journal."

"No, it won't," Duck said and wiped her nose with the back of her hand. "There's nothing interesting to tell."

"Nothing doesn't make much of a story. Can't you think of something for me to write in the journal?" Jenny said. Her blue eyes flashed. She twisted a long thin strand of hair between her fingers.

"You're the writer, not me," said Duck. "Scribbling's a far sight easier than riding behind cattle all day."

"I do not scribble," Jenny said disdainfully. "I write."

Fanny snapped the flour-sack rag and hung it on a wagon-wheel spoke to dry. "Why don't you read aloud what you've got so far? Maybe I can help you think of something."

Jenny smoothed the page of the journal, an expensive bound book with a brown cardboard cover and marbled-edge pages that Father had bought back in Illinois especially for the trip. Everything Jenny wrote in the journal had to be approved by Father, who was as severe a taskmaster about recording the day's events as he was about plowing, horse breaking, or corn planting. Father read every entry and checked it to make sure she had included correct locations and mileage.

Jenny cleared her throat. " 'Independence Rock is in many places covered with names of visitors to this place. The earliest one was dated 1838. A great deal were dated 1850 and 1851, but the majority were 1852. Jenny and Fanny were first to climb the rock and write their names very big and black.' "

Duck made a face at her sister. Jenny did not pay any attention to her and kept reading. " 'We crossed the Sweetwater twice and came out on the same side. We had to raise our wagon beds six inches by which we managed to keep our "plunder" from being damaged. Find better grass than we have had for some days. In spite of lack of wood, Fanny was able to bake fine biscuits using sage roots. She is a wise, unselfish traveler, dedicated to everyone's welfare.' "

"You weren't first," Duck said quietly.

" 'To the top.' That's what I said," Jenny replied and tapped her pencil against the journal's edge. She gave Duck a superior smirk.

Duck frowned. "You didn't mention anything about the view," she said in a low voice. "You didn't say anything about climbing so high we could see all the way back to Castle Hill."

Jenny drew something small and illegible in the margin of the journal, then smudged it away with a damp finger. "Father said not to mention what happened at Castle Hill again," Jenny said slowly.

"Why?" Duck asked.

"You ask too many questions, Duck," Fanny said severely. Then she turned to Jenny and smiled. "I liked what you wrote. Especially the part about me and the biscuits. 'Wise, unselfish, and dedicated to everyone's welfare.' That was very lovely."

"One day many people will read this," Jenny said.

"Who?" Duck asked. "Relatives back home?"

"No. Lots of people. People we don't know," Jenny insisted. "This is going to be published."

Duck still felt confused. "In the *Alton Times*?"

"No, not in a newspaper, foolish child. In a book," Jenny replied. "My name is going to be on the cover. I'll be famous."

"Really?" Fanny said in a bright, hopeful

voice. "Then I'll be famous, too. People will read about me. 'Wise, unselfish, and dedicated to everyone's welfare.' I'll be an inspiration."

Duck didn't think she could stand listening to her proud, cheating sisters another moment. "I'm leaving," she said.

"Take this to Wilkie," Fanny said and handed her the bowl of precious bread and milk.

Duck hurried to the next wagon. In the darkness beyond she heard the cattle cropping the grass and the snuffle of contented horses. She knocked her secret knock on the wooden side of Mother's Wagon. "Wilkie?" she called. "I've brought you something nice to eat." She scrambled up inside the wagon.

How strange it seemed not to see Mother there on the feather bed! A candle burned in a jar on one of the wagon shelves. In the flickering shadows Wilkie looked sad and pale and lonely. He sat surrounded by the bright tulip quilt Grandmother had made so many years ago. His face was pinched and serious. She knew he must be missing Mother. "Where's Chat?" Duck asked as cheerfully as she could. "I thought she was keeping you company. Have you been here by yourself for very long?"

Wilkie struggled to sit up. "Chat's coming back." Even though he was only three years old, he seemed much older because he could speak so well.

Duck sat down beside her little brother. Always sickly, Wilkie had been the special delight of Mother. "Look," Duck said. "Here's something tasty. Fanny made you your favorite."

"You eat it. I'm not hungry," he said.

Wilkie was special. Father made sure Fanny had the right ingredients to cook him special puddings, and he never scolded Wilkie when he didn't finish his dinner. Because Wilkie was a boy and the youngest and most fragile, he was the only one who was allowed to hold Father's silver pocket watch. Wilkie could not run and play like other children, so Father never made him do any work on the farm—not even feed the chickens.

In spite of his unusual treatment, Wilkie wasn't resented by Duck or her brothers and sisters. They never picked on him. Instead, they marveled at his sweetness—especially when he was obviously in terrible pain. There was something about the kind, sad boy that made him seem as if he were from another world. Grandmother called him Angel Eyes, and even Father admitted that Wilkie might have some special gift. A month ago near Loup River Ford on the Platte, no one believed it when Wilkie said the favorite old mare, Sukey, would wander off and drown. And sure enough, she did. Duck wished she had heeded her brother's advice and watched Sukey more closely. It was as if he could see the future.

Thinking about Sukey gave Duck an idea. Maybe Wilkie could help her. "Wilkie?" she asked. "Do you think I'll ever do anything remarkable?"

Wilkie looked at her as if he did not understand what she was talking about.

Duck cleared her throat and studied her brother's face carefully. "Do you think I'll ever be famous?"

"No," said a voice in the doorway. It was Kit and she was laughing.

"What's so funny?" Duck demanded. She could feel her face burning bright red.

"You'll never be famous or do anything the least bit important. Look at you. Your face is dirty. Your hair is uncombed. Your nails haven't been trimmed in months. You're a disgrace," Kit said in a superior voice. "What are you doing here?" She climbed into the wagon with a basin of water.

"I brought some food for Wilkie," Duck replied.

"Feeding Wilkie's *my* job," Kit said. "He's not hungry because he's got a fever. Will you get out of my way? I have to bathe his forehead."

Duck looked anxiously at her brother. She watched Kit wring out a rag in the basin and placed it on Wilkie's forehead. "Is he going to be all right?" Duck whispered.

"Oh, yes. I think so. He's had fevers before," said Kit. She glanced critically at her own hands, which were calloused and tanned from the sun. "I wish Father let us bring our gloves. My hands will never be as pretty as they once were."

"What do you want with gloves?" Duck asked. "They'd only get worn out and ruined out here. Pretty soon you'll be longing for a parasol."

"What's wrong with a parasol?"

"Nothing except that the first strong wind would blow you all the way back to Illinois."

"All the way home?" Wilkie asked. "Will you take me, too?"

Duck bit her lip and looked at her sister. Kit quickly wrung out the rag again. "Don't you know Duck's just talking nonsense?" Kit said.

"I want to go home," Wilkie said. He began quietly weeping.

"What's the matter, Wilkie? Are you feeling very bad?" Duck asked. She wished Mother were here. Mother would know what to do.

"We'll never get to Oregon," he blurted, "if we keep camping in the same place every night."

Kit glanced in confusion at her sister.

"Oh, no, Wilkie," Duck said as cheerfully as she could. "It just looks like we're camping in the same place. We're actually moving on and on every day."

Wilkie sniffed. "We are?"

Kit breathed a sigh of relief. "Everything does look the same out here." She placed the rag on Wilkie's forehead and turned to Duck. "Why did you talk about Illinois and make him cry?" she hissed. "You know he isn't well."

"Sorry," Duck mumbled. "Can I help you do something?"

"No," Kit replied. "You're too dirty to help be Wilkie's nurse. Take this bread and milk back to Fanny. No sense wasting it."

Duck picked up the untouched bowl of food. She looked sadly at her little brother, whose eyes were closed now. "Good night, Wilkie," she said softly. She left the wagon and jumped to the ground. Maybe Kit was right. Maybe she'd never do anything important. She'd never be famous. As she walked back to the provision wagon, she used her fingers to shovel the soggy bread into her mouth. Then she gulped the last of the milk. Somehow the delicacy didn't taste as good as she'd imagined. She wiped her lips with the back of her hand and left the empty bowl beside the washtub.

Duck sighed. She felt sad and lonely. She'd go and talk to Maggie, that was what she'd do. Maggie always made her feel better.

Chapter 5

"All the tigers are gone!" someone called out in a singsong voice in the darkness around the circle of wagons.

"All the tigers are gone!" came the reply a few feet away.

"Harvey? Sonny?" Duck said. "That you?"

Harvey lunged out of a shadow, snarling and howling like a wild beast. He curled his fingers like claws and gnashed his terrible teeth. "We need another person for our game. Want to play?" he asked. "I'm the tiger."

Harvey was clever, always thinking up new schemes to pass the time. He was a full head taller than Duck and twice as strong. He tolerated Duck because he admired good riders — in addition to good shots, dirty talkers, tough fighters, and anyone who could endure pain and not cry. Even though Harvey was in the middle of the family, he had power. He was the oldest boy, after all, and he never let his sisters forget it.

"Have you seen Maggie?" Duck asked.

"She was just here and said she'd be right back," Harvey replied. "I don't know where she went. Play with us, Duck, till she comes. We need somebody to help feed the tiger."

"Why not ask Kit?" Duck suggested.

"We can't use Kit," Harvey replied with contempt. "You know she's afraid of the dark. You play, Duck. We need you."

"All right," Duck said reluctantly. "Just until Maggie comes. I have to talk to her."

"Go hide with Sonny," Harvey said. "Home base is over there by that boulder."

Duck slipped away among the shadows. Someone coughed. "Sonny?" she whispered. "You don't sound so good."

"I'm fine," Sonny replied gruffly. Through the darkness Duck could imagine Sonny sitting hunched on the ground with his winglike shoulder blades showing. Unlike Harvey, skinny Sonny wasn't the least bit athletic. However, he never complained and he was always his oldest brother's most devoted lieutenant. "Be quiet so we can hear the signal," he told Duck.

Sure enough, there came a terrific tiger growl. "Scatter!" Sonny whispered.

Duck knew the rules. She and her brother separated and hurried into the darkness. Carefully she approached rocks and trees, calling out every so often, "All the tigers are gone."

Suddenly she heard Chat scream. She had been captured by the pouncing tiger and now would serve as the tiger's assistant.

"All the tigers are gone!" Duck called out the reassuring lie.

Nearby she heard someone talking. Who was it? She couldn't tell because of the darkness. Quietly she crept toward the voices. As she came closer, she was aware of the low drone of a man speaking. She recognized the voice. It was John MacDonald's. She took a few more steps. From the darkness came a piercing, twittering giggle—the same ridiculous sound Duck had heard after they crossed the Sweetwater earlier that day. Maggie! Duck stood frozen, listening. What was wrong with her sister?

"Maggie?" Duck called cautiously into the darkness. "We're waiting for you to play the Tiger Game with us. Come on."

"I don't want to play," Maggie replied. "Go away."

Duck cleared her throat. "Can I talk to you for a minute?"

"No," Maggie replied.

Duck heard John MacDonald mumble something. Her sister's piercing giggle filled the air again.

Duck couldn't bear the horrible noise. She clenched her fists. She wanted to shout something awful. Somehow she couldn't. Why was Maggie acting so strange? She didn't have time to play. She didn't have time to talk. Duck turned and stumbled against an overturned tin washtub.

"Walk much, Grace?" John MacDonald called.

Duck fled. She ran back to the Salon Wagon and buried her head in her blanket to escape her sister's unnatural laughter.

❧

On the plaines
July 20 1852

To Mary Augusta Brown

dear couzin it is with pleasure that I take
this opportunity to write you a few lines to
let you know how we get along We seen
the rocky Mountains faraway yet that look
like dirty clouds Mostly we follow the val-
leys and recross Dry Sandy and Little
sandy and Big Sandy which are troublesome rivers a very small part of the journey
I enjoy very well but the greater part of it
is very tiresome and hard I ride on horseback most of the way I seen a great many
curiosities on the road It is a very grand
sight indeed for any person that is not used
to it there are in some places sand and dust
which are hot enough to roast eggs and is
very annoying indeed Most annoying of all
is my sister Maggie which you may recall
was my best sister but now I don't understand anything about her no more She dont

talk to me or play with me the way she
used to I am writing to you since you are
my best friend back home maybe you have
some ideas what can cause such a change
in a person it makes me sad I don't have
nobody to talk to except you in letters I
cannot be runing about in the grass lot and
pasture and rolling down the Corn in the
crib like we used to I cannot be a running
to Grandfathers with the news papers nothing seems like home here to me Tell
Tommy that he must not forget to write to
me when we get to Oregon I must bring
my letter to a close give my love to Aunt
poly and grandmother and write soon

> Yours affectionately
> H.L.S. (Duck)

&

It was a hot, dusty afternoon on July 24,
about five miles northeast of American Falls. As
Duck rode along on Shuttleback, she checked
to make sure the letter to her cousin was still
safe inside her pocket. She had followed the
strange phrasing of her older sisters' letters

home and hoped it looked impressive. Not until they reached Old Fort Boise, a couple hundred miles away, would she have the opportunity to send the letter back to Illinois with travelers returning east on the Oregon Trail. Until then, she had to make sure the letter didn't get lost or fall into the wrong hands. *What if one of my sisters finds it and reads it?* She didn't want to give Maggie the satisfaction of knowing just how miserable she had made Duck feel.

Duck sighed. Since they'd left Independence Rock, she'd discovered no opportunity for the kind of adventure Uncle Levi had described. Nothing exciting ever seemed to happen. No Indians came to visit. No bandits attacked. There had been no buffalo stampedes, no runaway wagons. Hour after hour the merciless wind blew dirt and flies straight into Duck's face as she rode Shuttleback and herded cattle. Grit coated her teeth and covered her hair. *Adventures await, Uncle Levi said. But where?*

Duck squinted into the bright, blinding light and yawned. *How pleasant it would be to ride in a wagon. Someplace soft and shady.* Just ahead she could see the Salon Wagon, which was being driven by cranky Al Critchfield.

Ordinarily, Critchfield whipped and drove the oxen far too fast. "Flogging animals is not only wholly unnecessary," Father constantly reminded Critchfield, "it is cruel. I will not tolerate it."

For once, impatient Critchfield was taking his time. The three teams of oxen—Buck and Bright, Bally and Bob, Holly and Berry—veered from one side of the pockmarked road to the other. They moved so slowly, Duck wondered if Critchfield were nodding off in the wagon seat. She was sure he wouldn't notice if she tied Shuttleback to the back of the wagon and climbed in for a short nap among the comforters. Duck sidled up to the wagon, pulled Shuttleback to a halt, and dismounted. It wasn't difficult for her to walk along, tie the reins to the back, and hop inside.

When she climbed in, she nearly jumped right out again. Sitting there among the bedding and clothing were Fanny and Jenny. "Duck, what do you think you're doing?" Fanny demanded.

Duck gulped.

"Aren't you supposed to be watching cattle?" Jenny said. She busily arranged several pieces of paper on the top of a chest of clothing.

Duck had to think fast. She stuck out her foot. "My shoe's worn practically through. And Shuttleback's getting saddle sores. So I'm giving her a rest. I'll only be here a little while."

"I should hope so," Fanny said and sniffed.

"If Father catches you loafing again, he'll be furious," Jenny added.

"Why can you ride in the wagon and I can't?" Duck demanded angrily.

"Because you get to rest all you want when we reach camp while I have to spend hours cooking," Fanny replied.

"And I have to write," Jenny said in a superior voice.

Duck snorted. "Writing's not very hard."

"Well, then, maybe you can help me," Jenny said. "Father said we're to write to Grandfather. If we get the letters done soon enough, we can leave them at Fort Boise."

Duck did not feel like helping Jenny do anything—much less write letters. "I'd really like to get some sleep," Duck replied in a sullen voice.

"We'd all like to sleep," Fanny announced. "But that's not the point. We need to finish these letters and you're going to help. If you don't think you can manage, perhaps Father can convince you."

"All right," Duck grumbled. Her vision of a peaceful, shady nap vanished.

Jenny handed Duck a piece of paper and a stubby pencil. "I've already started a letter. See?" She held up a half page filled with neat penmanship. "Now get to work. Today's the twenty-fourth of July. Be sure to write that." Jenny sounded just like Miss Alicia Mark, the insipid Illinois schoolteacher Duck had despised.

Duck sighed. She wrote the date at the top of the page. Then she stared at the rest of the empty page. What should she say? How homesick she felt for Illinois? Thinking of Grandfather and Mary Augusta Brown and her other cousins and aunts and uncles gave her a dull ache in the middle of her chest.

How she missed Grandfather! Gentle hearted and generous, he was the one person who did not holler when Duck and Mary Augusta slid down his corncrib or ran through the hay meadow performing very unladylike leaps. Grandfather had taught them how to hoot like barred owls—a call that sounded like: "Who-cooks-for-you? Who-cooks-for-you-all?"

He showed them how to carve cardinals from soft pieces of wood. When would she ever see him or Mary Augusta Brown again?

"The letter won't write itself," Fanny said, leaning forward to inspect Duck's empty page. "I hope you're not going to waste that expensive paper."

"I'm thinking. This is my first letter to Grandfather," Duck said. "Leave me alone."

"We have to tell him," Jenny said slowly. "We have to tell him about Mother."

Duck's shoulders sagged. *Mother.* She could always count on Mother for comfort, no matter what. Mother had never said, "Go away" or "Leave me alone." Everything would be different if she were still here. Father wouldn't seem so harsh. Her sisters wouldn't seem so critical and quarrelsome. If Mother were still alive, maybe Maggie would be sweet and attentive. She'd cut Duck's bread into the shape of butterflies and make her laugh. She'd listen to Duck's secret fears. Now Maggie ignored Duck. The only person Maggie ever wanted to be with was John MacDonald. Nobody in the world seemed to exist for her except him.

Everything was better when Mother was alive. Everything.

"What should we say to Grandfather?" Fanny asked.

"He'll be so upset," Duck said. "Poor Grandfather."

"Jenny, why don't you share what you have so far?" Fanny said. "You're the family writer."

As usual, Jenny was only too happy to display her great talent. " 'My Dear Grandfather,' " she read. " 'As Father at present has no taste for writing, it becomes my duty to commence the (at this time painful task) of writing to you. Since we last addressed you, the mysterious, relentless hand of Death has visited us, and we are now mourning the decease of our beloved Mother!' "

Fanny clasped her hands together. "Isn't that beautiful? Here, let me read what I have so far. It's a short but elegant beginning: 'Dear Grandfather: It is with pleasure that I embrace this opportunity of writing a few lines to let you know how we are getting along . . .' How does that sound?"

Jenny was deep in thought, scribbling away. Fanny sighed and went back to writing. Finally

Duck, too, took up her pencil and, in spite of the lurching wagon, managed to copy her sister's beginning: " 'Dear Grandfather: It is with pleazur I . . .' " Suddenly she thought of something else important. "Shouldn't we ask him what happened to Watch?"

"That smelly old dog?" Fanny said.

"He was a good watchdog. And he was loyal," Duck replied. "Remember how he followed us all the way to the Illinois River and just stood there and barked and barked as if his heart would break? And then Father shouted at him to go back to Grandfather's. I wonder if he ever did. Poor Watch. I miss him."

"Well, I don't," Jenny replied. "He had fleas and ticks and who knows what else in his mangy fur."

"Father said we could take nothing along that wasn't worth less than a dollar a pound," Fanny said and sniffed. "There wasn't room for Watch."

"I doubt Watch was worth a dollar," Jenny said and laughed.

Duck scowled at her hard-hearted sisters. She hunched forward and scribbled a few more words. " 'I have went through a great manny changes and difficulties, since I last saw you and

I now know what I never knew before that is to be bereft of a Mothers advice. . . .' "

Stealthily Jenny reached into her stout cloth sewing bag where she kept her needle and thimble and spools of thread. She slipped out a small, battered blue-backed book and furtively flipped through the pages. Duck recognized the book immediately. "Does Father know you smuggled that school speller on the wagon?" she announced. "I doubt it's worth more than a dollar a pound."

Jenny's face flushed. She struggled to stuff the small book back inside her sewing bag. "I don't care if you know," she said with great confidence, although she was clearly flustered. "If I'm going to be a famous writer one day, I need to learn at least another hundred words."

Duck glanced at Fanny, the enforcer. What did she think of her sister's breaking Father's rule? Fanny cocked her head to one side and smiled at Duck with a patronizing grin.

"Words are precious," Jenny continued. "You can do anything with words. Why I plan to—"

Without warning the wagon lurched, crashed, and rolled.

Chapter 6

The girls screamed. Duck went flying. She slammed against something hard. There was a wrenching crack. Darkness. She couldn't breathe. She couldn't move. Her arms and legs seemed to be pinned under something. Was she dead? No. She heard a shout and someone cursing loudly. Someone who sounded like Al Critchfield.

At last, excitement! Was this the adventure she had been waiting for? Duck struggled to free herself, convinced that this was her chance to be brave and bold. She wriggled but could not move her arms. How was she going to do something outstanding and remarkable tangled up in a comforter?

Somewhere nearby she could hear her sisters crying. "Fanny? Jenny?" Duck called. "Don't worry. I'll help you." With all her might, Duck crawled out from under a pile of blankets. She kicked a barrel off her legs and slithered out of the wagon wreckage into bright sunlight. She saw an arm. She grabbed it and pulled out Jenny, who looked more shaken than hurt. "Can you move your legs?" Duck asked.

Jenny nodded. Her skirt was up almost over her head, but she was too dazed to notice. Duck shuffled around the back of the wagon to look for Fanny. She was surprised and delighted instead to find Shuttleback, safe and sound. Luckily, the worn rawhide strap attached to the horse had snapped when the wagon flipped. Shuttleback nibbled grass near a heap of clothing as unconcerned as if nothing at all had happened.

"Duck, did you find Fanny?" Jenny asked. She wobbled on her feet and began to pull away a toppled comforter and a featherbed.

A loud *crack, crack, crack* filled the air. Duck was horrified to see Al Critchfield whipping the oxen. The three teams lowed and stumbled to their knees.

"Stop!" Duck screamed.

Critchfield pretended not to hear her.

"What do you think you're doing?" Father shouted. He grabbed Critchfield so forcefully, the little man dropped the whip. Father snatched the whip and waved it in front of Critchfield's face. "Your bad driving caused a wagon wreck. Right into a hole. And now you beat my oxen? What did I tell you I'd do if I ever caught you flogging my teams again?"

"I don't care what you told me," bragged Critchfield, even though he cowered on the ground like a lame grasshopper.

While Father and Al Critchfield exchanged insults, Uncle Levi helped the girls paw through the wreckage. "Are you all right?" he asked Duck and Jenny.

"We're fine, but we can't find Fanny," Duck said.

"Help! Help!" Fanny stuck her head out of the back of the wagon. "Oh, Lord," she cried, "come here quick!"

"Hadn't you better skip calling God and call on some of the company instead?" Uncle Levi asked, smiling.

Fanny clearly did not think Uncle Levi was very funny. She pulled herself out of the debris and stood up in as ladylike a posture as she could manage.

"Where is it?" Jenny hissed. She was on all fours hunting through the boxes and barrels and blankets. "Where is it?"

"You lose something?" Duck asked. Instinctively she patted her pocket to make sure the letter to Mary Augusta was still safe. *Thank goodness!*

Jenny did not answer. She just kept tossing aside blankets and pillows. Now Duck understood. The blue speller. Without a word, she and Fanny joined Jenny's search. "What are you girls looking for?" Uncle Levi demanded.

"Nothing," Duck hissed. She gave Uncle Levi a pleading look.

"A very important nothing, that's certain," Uncle Levi said.

"We'll have to lose a day to make repairs," Father announced. "This is a terrible waste of time. A whole day or more lost—and not much water. As for you, Critchfield, you can be horsewhipped or you can leave this wagon company right now."

Critchfield stood up, his fists on his hips, his

sharp elbows out. Slowly he moved one hand toward the inside of his vest.

"Hold it right there," John MacDonald ordered. He held his rifle barrel between Critchfield's shoulder blades. "Drop that gun, you trifling fool."

Critchfield froze. He did as he was told. Father took the pistol and handed it to Uncle Levi. Uncle Levi held the pistol gingerly between two fingers. Meanwhile the rest of the hired men had gathered around the tipped wagon. All eyes were on Father. What would he do?

Finally Uncle Levi coughed and broke the strained silence. "Tucker," he said bravely, "it's not fair to leave a man on the trail with no provisions. He'll die out there."

Father would not be dissuaded. "Critchfield has cost me enough already. I'll give him his fair share of rations, then he's on his way. Or he can be horsewhipped and stay. What's your choice, Critchfield?"

Critchfield went into a fury. He kicked a fallen featherbed and then kicked a wagon wheel. The more the other men laughed at him, the more ferociously he attacked the barrels, boxes, and blankets.

"Your featherbed, Father!" Fanny cried. She rushed to protect the bedding. "He's kicking your featherbed!"

The other men laughed even louder. "Easier to beat up a man's featherbed than a man," John MacDonald joked.

Critchfield gave Fanny and her sisters a dark, threatening look. Then he turned to Father. "I'll not be horsewhipped," he snarled. "Give me my share of food and water and I'll leave."

Fanny dragged the featherbed a few feet from the wagon. She sat on the ground and began to sob. Duck tried to comfort her. "There, there!" she said. "Everything will be fine. You'll see."

But Fanny would not stop crying.

"Is it Mother?" Duck turned to Jenny and whispered. "Is Fanny crying because she's sad about Mother?"

Jenny shook her head, but refused to speak. She helped arrange the other fallen bedding into a pile. Father stormed away. Huffing and puffing, Critchfield followed to collect his cask of water and grub. As soon as everyone drifted out of sight, Jenny leaned close to Fanny and said, "Let's see if they're still all right."

In utter amazement, Duck watched as her

two sisters used Jenny's sewing scissors to cut away a little space in the featherbed cover—just big enough for Fanny to slip her hand inside. She pulled something out. It gleamed bright blue and white in the sunlight.

"What is that?" Duck whispered.

"One of the Dutch plates that once belonged to Mother," Jenny said. "There are six of them all together."

Duck felt confused. "What are they doing sewed inside Father's featherbed?"

"Remember George?" Jenny asked.

Duck nodded. "Fanny's beau back home."

"That's the one," Jenny said. "When Father had the auction back in Illinois, he made us sell everything. Even the Dutch plates. George felt sorry for Fanny. He knew those plates were supposed to be part of her hope chest—the things she'd need after she was married. So he bought the plates at the auction and he gave them back to Fanny. Father never knew. Then Fanny and Mother turned smuggler and sewed them into Father's featherbed, packing them so well that they would not be broken or crushed."

"Mother was a smuggler?" Duck said in disbelief. She had never seen Mother defy Father in her life. She looked at Fanny in amazement, scarcely able to believe that Fanny, too, would ever purposefully break one of Father's sacred rules.

"You must promise not to tell him, Duck," Jenny said softly.

Duck nodded solemnly. Now she understood. Jenny and Fanny had been keeping each other's smuggled treasures a secret from Father. And now Duck knew about *both* the hidden speller and the Dutch plates. She smiled. For the first time, she didn't feel small and weak and puny in the presence of her oldest sisters. She felt powerful.

July 24

*O*wing *to the carelessness of one of the drivers the wagon in which my self and sisters were riding ran into a deep mud hole and upset; we were very much frightened but fortunately did not get hurt The wagon contained chests of clothing and feather beds with which it was heavily loaded; There happened to be no serious damage done; The wagon bows were all broken; After having been told to leave the train or do better he took French leave of us and we have not* *seen or heard of him since. We remained in camp as our cattle were quite weak and the grass in the bottom is good; Our best hunter went out to look for game. A man died in the afternoon in a train near us, with the mountain fever They buried him in the evening; The weather is excessively hot.*

—Jenny

Chapter

7

One of our bravest and best hunters, J. MacDonald, told me this story of his hunt of several weeks ago, which I include here

—Maggie

"When the camp was lying still, I went tramping . . . until the sun began to approach toward the western horizon . . . we discovered the object of our search namely a band of Buffalo . . . after crawling for Conciderable distance . . . keeping a small bunch of greesewood between us and the buffalo we succeeded in giting with in rifle shot . . . the wounded animal ran a few yards and stopped . . . had to wait for him

to die not daring to approach him while he had life
for he was rather a ferotious looking and acting sort
of anamal . . . we then dressed the buffalo and each
of us took a back load and started for our camp . . .
The red sky of the West turned grey like the other
parts of the Horizon and the little stars grew bright
and twinkled in the distance . . . the moon cold and
pale . . . as we passed along Hard beaten trails . . .
the smell of fresh meat caused the wolves to howl and
follow our track."

The caravan was pulled into a circle. The rest
of the day was spent repairing the wagon. To pass
the time while work was being done by two other
hired men, John MacDonald took his rifle to
search for game along the Portneuf River. Father
scouted ahead to see if he might be able to rendez-
vous with another wagon train willing to trade
him a team of oxen for cash. He promised to be
back by the next morning. Meanwhile, Duck and
her sisters aired out bedding by draping blankets
and featherbeds atop the wagons.

That evening even a smoky fire of woody
sagebrush failed to keep away the biting mosquitoes. Duck stood before the fire, a blanket
wrapped around her shoulders and head. She

swatted away the bugs and listened to the wind scouring the sage and sand plains. Her stomach growled. That evening she had eaten her entire plate of beans, but she still felt hungry. Uneasily she glanced into the shadows and wondered where Critchfield might be at this very moment. Had he wandered far ahead? *What if he's nearby, waiting for a chance for revenge now that Father's gone and can't protect us?*

Suddenly a loud whoop filled the air. Two hired men dived for their rifles. Duck grabbed Maggie's hand and together they pulled little Chat under the wagon. "It's scalpers for sure!" Maggie hissed.

"Do you think so?" Duck asked. *Two adventures in one day!* Any minute she expected to hear guns blazing, shouts, and a chance to do something heroic. She didn't know what exactly, but she was sure it would be something amazing and remarkable.

Chat started to cry. Duck held her hands over her littlest sister's eyes. But instead of Indians, out of the shadows stepped John MacDonald. Over his horse's back lay something brown with white and black markings.

"What are you doing? Trying to scare us to

death?" Uncle Levi demanded. "We thought you was Shoshone."

"Sorry," John replied. "I've brought fresh meat. Pronghorn antelope."

Duck crept out from beneath the wagon. She was surprised to see John walking toward her, tugging something behind him. "Look what I found for you, Duck," he said.

Duck gasped when she saw the frisky little fawn with soft, dark eyes and spindly legs. The young pronghorn had a wavy brown coat and pointed ears that stood straight up. His head came just past Duck's waist. The dainty fawn stood and looked around, unafraid of Duck and her brothers and sisters, who crowded around it.

"I'm sorry to say I'm responsible for making this little fellow an orphan," John said.

"Poor, poor little dear." Jenny stroked his head between two little button horns. "He looks so delicate. His eyes are too big. His legs are too long. He looks like an exaggerated drawing—not like a real live animal at all—don't you think, Maggie?"

Maggie did not seem the least impressed. She

looked at John with angry eyes. "You brought this for Duck?" she demanded.

John nodded and winked at Duck. "I thought she could use some cheering."

Duck held out her hand, absolutely entranced. The pronghorn licked her fingers eagerly, just as Watch had done. "He's beautiful," she murmured. "He's the most beautiful thing I ever saw in my life."

"Well, you might not think he's so beautiful when he grows up to be a hundred-pound buck that knocks you flat with his horns," Uncle Levi said and laughed. "Then he'll run off fast as the wind. Ever seen a herd of pronghorn run? Looks like one continuous wave across the plains. Fastest things alive out here."

"Maggie," Harvey announced for everyone to hear, "did you know your face is as red as a tomato?"

Duck glanced at her sister. *Now what's wrong?*

"I'll go get the pronghorn some water," Maggie said quickly. She ran to the water barrel.

"How come she's so hopping mad?" Sonny grumbled. "You'd think she'd be happy we have a new pet."

Duck shrugged. *Maybe she wants the pronghorn.*

Maybe she's mad because John gave him to me. Duck smiled. For the second time that day she felt strangely powerful.

By the time Maggie came back, she seemed calmer. Her face wasn't flushed anymore. She offered the pronghorn a pan of water. He lapped it up eagerly. "He can have some of my dinner, too," Maggie said. She handed Duck a piece of biscuit from her pocket.

Duck looked suspiciously at the biscuit and then at her sister. Maggie flashed a secret look at John. Then she smiled at Duck. Her expression seemed warm and genuine. "Take it," Maggie said. "I want you to have this."

Maybe she's saying she's sorry. "Thank you," Duck said happily. She accepted the biscuit. The pronghorn ate every last crumb. When he was finished, she patted his soft back. Maggie patted his soft back, too.

"What should we call him?" Duck asked Maggie. She felt pleased to share her good fortune with her sister, especially if it meant that Maggie might pay attention to her again.

"Lucky's a good name," Jenny suggested.

"Too girlish," Harvey complained. "He needs

a name that's rough and tough. What about Rocky for Rocky Mountains?"

"Let Duck decide the name," Maggie said. "He belongs to her."

Fanny stepped closer. She inspected the pronghorn, but she did not touch him. "A pet is a lot of work," she said to Duck. "When Father comes back, he may not let you keep it."

"I'll help Duck take care of the poor little orphan," Maggie said. "Father won't be inconvenienced."

Good old Maggie. Duck glanced up defiantly at her oldest sister. "Father will let me keep the pronghorn if you don't say anything nasty about him and sour him on the idea. A fawn like this is special. A living breathing thing that's much more fragile than a—"

"Than what?" Fanny demanded, her eyes narrowing.

"Than some dumb old china, for instance," Duck said. She arched one eyebrow. "I think Father will agree with me on that."

Fanny blushed. For once, she seemed unable to think of a nasty reply.

"I don't know what you're talking about," Harvey said. He brushed the fawn's coat with his hand. "I'd say this little fellow's pretty tough. He doesn't look breakable as china. And if Father asks about the pronghorn, don't worry, Duck. I'll convince him you should keep it. Father listens to me."

"Aren't you the big man!" Jenny said, laughing.

Harvey paid no attention to her. He crouched on the ground and held the antelope's face with his two hands. He gazed into the pronghorn's eyes. "Duck, if he's going to grow up and be so fast, why don't you call him Dash?"

"What about Mercury or Hermes? They flew fast as the wind. And a Roman or Greek god's name sounds very literary," Jenny said.

"Those names are too fussy," Harvey said. "What do you think, Duck? You decide."

"Dash," Duck said. "I like that." Happily she led the little pronghorn away with the rope to make him a proper bed. "We have to find someplace safe for him to sleep," she told Maggie, who tagged along—much to Duck's delight.

"That's right," Maggie said. "We don't want coyotes or Al Critchfield to bother Dash tonight."

"Do you think Critchfield's still out there?" Duck asked anxiously.

"I'm sure he's miles away by now," Maggie said with a serious face. "I was more worried about Father coming back in the dark and stumbling over the pronghorn by accident." She winked at Duck and they both burst into laughter.

The two girls piled up some dry bunches of grass under the Salon Wagon. They covered the dried grass with two old burlap feed bags. Duck and Maggie sat under the wagon with the pronghorn, who seemed very content in his cozy new bed. *Just like old times.* Duck felt so delighted to be with her sister, she was afraid to speak for fear the spell might be broken and Maggie might turn moody and mean and abandon her again.

"Is there anything for Dash's breakfast?" Maggie asked. "I gave him the only biscuit I had."

"I'll go see what I can find," Duck said, reluctant to leave. "Will you stay here and keep Dash company? I'll be right back." She hurried to the provision wagon to see what she might be able to find in the way of food. She reached her hand inside the barrel that contained hardtack. Only a few broken pieces remained.

"What do you think you're doing?" Fanny demanded as she came around the corner of the wagon.

"Getting some food for Dash," Duck said as calmly as she could. "The pronghorn is so little, he needs something easy to eat when he wakes up in the morning. I'm going to soak this cracker all night in a bit of water. It's just a little broken moldy piece, see?"

"You won't tell Father will you?" Fanny pleaded.

"About what?" Duck gave her sister an innocent look.

"You know," Fanny replied. "About the blue Dutch plates."

"As long as you keep your promise about the pronghorn," she said and smiled. Then she reached inside the barrel and took an extra piece of hardtack. She ran as fast as she could back to Maggie and Dash. To her surprise, she arrived just in time to see John MacDonald peeking under the wagon.

"Something wrong with Dash?" she asked nervously.

"The pronghorn seems fine," John replied. "I was just saying good night."

Duck scrambled on all fours into the shadows under the wagon. It was too dark to see Dash or her sister's face.

"Sweet dreams, John!" Maggie's voice rang out.

She's still in a good mood. "Good night," Duck said. She listened as John's footsteps grew fainter and fainter.

"Isn't he wonderful?" Maggie asked.

"He's the best pronghorn I ever saw," Duck said enthusiastically.

Maggie laughed. "No, I mean John. Isn't he wonderful?"

"Yes, I suppose so. He gave me Dash." Duck sighed. *Can't we talk about something interesting?*

"Do you think he misses her?"

"Who?" Duck replied. *Not John again.*

"Dash," Maggie said. "Do you think Dash misses his mother?"

Duck brightened. "Yes, of course. Animals have feelings, too."

"Do you think about Mother very much?"

Duck took a deep breath. "Every minute. What about you?"

"Sometimes I wonder if the ache might never go away the rest of my life," Maggie said quietly. "Better get some sleep now." She covered Duck with a burlap sack.

Duck closed her eyes. She tried to think how wonderful it was to share Dash with Maggie. How wonderful it was to have her sister back again. *Just like old times.* But somehow, no matter how hard she tried, she could not feel completely happy. *The ache might never go away.* She rested her cheek against the soft, warm motherless pronghorn. "Sweet dreams," she whispered.

Chapter

8

WHEN DISTURBED by the traveler, the pronghorn antelope will circle around him with the speed of the wind, but does not stop until it reaches some prominent position whence it can survey the country on all sides, and nothing seems to escape its keen vision. They will sometimes stand for a long time and look at a man, provided he does not move or go out of sight; but if he goes behind a hill with the intention of passing around and getting nearer to the pronghorn, he will never find the pronghorn again in the same place.

—THE PRAIRIE TRAVELER

Father returned early the next morning. Unfortunately, he had found no travelers willing to trade him cash for extra oxen. "Chain up! Roll out!" he announced. By late afternoon the caravan set off again. To make up for lost time and to avoid the heat of midday, Father insisted the wagons keep moving through the evening and into the night. Rocky hills made the road treacherous. The thirsty, lagging teams were urged on by their tired drivers. Everyone hoped for water ahead. But none could be found.

July 26

We found the roads very bad; being over sand and sage plains The weather is excessively hot & the dust so dence that it is with difficulty we can see our way.
—*Jenny*

It was very difficult to ride Shuttleback anywhere near the little pronghorn. Duck tried leading with a very long line, but Dash wasn't used to the arrangement and was quickly tangled up. When the little fawn came too close to Shuttleback, the ornery horse's ears flattened against her head. She had no motherly instincts, even though the pronghorn followed her faithfully.

In desperation Duck dismounted and led the pronghorn and horse to the camp equipment wagon and called inside for Maggie. "Dash is about to collapse. He can barely keep up," Duck said. "Look how his tongue is hanging from his mouth. His legs are too short to walk behind this big horse. And I'm afraid Shuttleback may kick him in the head. Is there some water left I can give him?"

"There's not even a drop left in the cask," Maggie said. "Chat and Wilkie are whimpering from thirst. No one seems to know how far to the next spring."

"What should we do about Dash?" Duck asked.

Maggie looked down at the poor struggling pronghorn. "Why don't you let me take care of him for a while? Maybe you can ride ahead and look for water." She went back inside the wagon, then reappeared. She jumped from the wagon with extra rags around her feet. "I was going to have to get out soon anyhow and walk to lighten the load. Father said there are steep hills ahead."

Gratefully Duck handed over Dash's line.

Ride ahead and look for water. Maybe this would be her chance to do something remarkable, something important everyone would appreciate. She guided Shuttleback to the front of the wagons. Father and the grumbling hired men were so busy chaining the back wheels of the wagons for the steep hill, they did not pay any attention when she rode past them and headed around the next bend. Even in the growing darkness, Shuttleback managed to pick her way carefully down the hill. One false move and she knew she'd go flying. *Was this what Uncle Levi meant by "No matter how hard"?*

The road wound around and around. Several times Shuttleback pitched forward and Duck nearly flew over the horse's head. But at the last minute she caught her balance and pulled herself back up into the saddle. Duck glanced quickly over her shoulder. She wondered what might be lurking in the darkness. What if Al Critchfield were somewhere in the shadows?

At the base of the third hill Duck thought she saw the unmistakable outline of willows and shrubs. A sure sign of water. She jumped down off the saddle. Listening hard, she tried to make out the sound of tinkling water. She sniffed.

Something smelled damp, decaying. A smell she remembered from countless swamps they had skirted before they reached the Mississippi. If only she had brought a lantern! Duck crouched on the ground and felt the dirt. Something sticky clung to her hand. Mud! Surely there had to be a spring nearby.

Excitedly she mounted Shuttleback, turned the big horse around, and headed back up the way they had come to tell the others. Wouldn't Father be pleased that she had found water? *This time all the hired men will cheer. No one will make fun of me.*

She remembered the poor little pronghorn with its lolling tongue and hurried faster. When she finally arrived back at the wagon train, she was exhausted and out of breath. "Water!" she cried. "Water ahead!"

"Where?" Father demanded.

"Down at the bottom of the third hill," she said.

The news quickly lifted everyone's spirits. But it still took nearly another two hours before the wagons with the back wheels chained finally creaked to the bottom of the last hill. Father and Uncle Levi held lanterns aloft and searched the rank reeds and bushes.

"Something smells wet, that's certain," Uncle Levi said.

John MacDonald shone a lantern under every clump bush. "Maybe we should name this Marsh Creek," he said. "The ground is muddy, but there's no standing water anywhere."

The oxen lowed pathetically. Chat cried out from the wagon, "Where's the water? Can I have some?"

"Duck, is this some kind of joke?" Fanny demanded.

"This is what happens when a girl attempts to do a man's job," Father replied. "We'll have to take shovels and dig. Perhaps water won't be too far down. The cattle can't go any farther. We'll have to camp here tonight."

Speechless, Duck clenched her fists in anger and disappointment. She'd tried to do something remarkable and failed again. Why couldn't Father see that she'd only been trying to help? He seemed more concerned about the oxen than he was about her. Was it her fault she was a girl? Why, if Harvey or Sonny had found this spot, Father would not have made fun of them. He never would have yelled at the boys in front of everyone.

She stomped away, leading Shuttleback by the reins. She picketed the horse near a scrubby patch of grass. She found Maggie and the pronghorn resting under the wagon. Duck and her sister listened to the men digging. Neither said anything for a long time.

"Don't pay Father any mind," Maggie said. "He's just tired and thirsty like everybody else. He doesn't know what he's saying."

"Yes, he does," Duck said bitterly. "If it weren't for you and Dash and Wilkie, I'd run away and never come back."

"Now, now," Maggie replied. "Everything will be fine, you'll see."

This time, however, Maggie's words of encouragement didn't brighten Duck's spirits. They only made her feel like a worse failure.

The next morning the oxen were given time to graze and lap up water from the shallow trench the men had dug with shovels. As soon as breakfast chores were finished, Maggie, Jenny, and Fanny worked on mending. "We'll keep an eye on Chat and Wilkie," Maggie told

Duck. "Why don't you go with the others and amuse yourselves for a while?"

Duck was not especially in the mood to amuse herself. But she joined Harvey, Sonny, and Kit as they went exploring beyond the campsite. Sure enough, the horrible smell, which seemed to be growing stronger with each passing hour, was coming from what appeared to be a large gray rock. As the children came closer, they realized that the rock was actually a dead gray mare. Nearby lay several dead oxen.

"What a smell!" Kit said, holding her nose.

"Aw! It's not that bad," Harvey insisted.

"Dare you to touch one of those dead oxen over there," Sonny said. "The one with the swollen stomach."

Nobody moved.

"I'm not scared," Duck said boldly. She could be just as brave as any boy. She dashed to the black ox, which seemed almost twice a living oxen's size. She gave it a pat and hurried back to her brothers. "There! That wasn't too awful."

Harvey did not like to appear a coward. With a swagger he walked over to the oxen. Just as he was about to give it a pat, the torn sole of his shoe caught on a rock and he went flying. Deftly he put his hands in front of himself to break the fall. When he crashed against the ox's black, tight belly, he bounced and sprang backward nearly a foot. He landed on his feet, knees bent, balanced and smiling as if he'd planned the whole thing.

Sonny applauded. "Nice trick!"

"Say," said Harvey, "this might make a game."

Kit looked doubtful. "What kind of a game?"

"The Ox Bouncing Game," said Harvey, smiling. "I just made it up. Here's how it goes." He drew a line in the dust with his foot a few feet from the dead ox. Then he made another line in the dust several feet away. "As soon as one of us gives the signal, somebody takes a running start, see?"

"What's the signal?" Sonny asked. He liked to know all the details before he joined in a game.

"You ask too many questions," said Harvey, exasperated. "Just watch." He took a running leap, and as soon as he reached the line, he flew through the air and landed against the swollen belly of the ox. The force of the blow caused him to bounce backward and land beyond the line he had drawn in the dirt. "See? I just beat my own record. Who can do better than that?"

"I can," Duck replied. She rubbed her hands together, crouched on the ground like the big boys did on the school grounds when they wanted a good running start.

"One . . . two . . . you know what to do!" Kit shouted.

Duck flew through the air, bounced against the oxen belly and landed even farther than Harvey.

"Nice bounce!" Kit said.

Duck bowed, pleased for once to have impressed her sister.

"It was just luck," said Sonny. "Harvey's the best."

"Now it's your turn, Sonny. Go ahead," said Harvey.

"Ready? One . . . two . . . you know what to do!" Kit shouted.

Sonny ran, flew through the air, and landed with a *whump!* on the dusty ground. He cradled his elbow and winced.

"Are you all right?" Duck asked.

"I'm fine," Sonny replied in a hurt, angry voice.

"Maybe this game is too dangerous," Kit said.

"It's perfectly safe," said Harvey, who considered himself an expert on daredevil pranks. "Look. I'll run even faster and I'll bounce even farther."

Over and over again for the rest of the morning, Duck and her sister and brothers played the Ox Bouncing Game. After a while they became so good at bouncing, they twisted themselves in midair or made little humorous, flapping hand motions as they soared. They laughed and bounced and laughed some more.

"Now I'm going to try something really amazing," boasted Harvey. "Nobody can beat this leap." He stood back as far as he could and ran as fast as he could straight for the oxen. But this time Harvey didn't bounce. *Gawp!* A loud pop filled the air, followed by an indescribable stench. "Help! I'm stuck!" screamed Harvey, sounding very far away. His head, neck and shoulders were lodged firmly inside the oxen carcass.

Duck laughed and laughed. Harvey looked so funny. His legs thrashed back and forth. His arms waved. Somehow Duck could not help thinking of someone wearing a gigantic ox for a hat. Kit did not think the sight—or the smell—was funny. She gagged, turned a shade of green, and vomited. Sonny rushed to Harvey's aid. He began tugging on his leg, but he was not strong enough to pull Harvey out. Duck had to help him. Together they finally managed to pull Harvey to freedom. His head was covered with slime and ooze. The rotten smell was so awful, both Duck and Sonny began to feel very sick.

Harvey staggered back to camp, followed by Duck, Kit, and Sonny. They all held their noses. "What happened to you?" Jenny shrieked.

Chat began to cry when she saw her brother. "Are you scalped?"

Because there was so little water available, it was almost impossible to scrub Harvey clean. "I hope you have learned your lesson from such a foolish dare," Fanny told Harvey. Slime still coated his hair, eyebrows, and ears, giving his spiky hair a strange dark green color.

"You're lucky Father's gone hunting with John," Maggie said. "He'll be furious when he finds out you've ruined your only set of clothes.

What on earth possessed you to mess about with something so disgusting as a dead ox?"

"It's all Duck's fault," Harvey grumbled. "She dared me."

"I did not," Duck insisted. "You thought of the game. You jumped because you wanted to."

"But you're the one who started it," Harvey said hotly. "You found the ox."

Fanny glared at Duck. "The same way you found the water that wasn't there and this awful campsite," she said with a snicker. "Look at you. You plague Father. You shirk your responsibilities. You are lazy and troublesome. Sometimes I can hardly believe that you are *my* sister."

Duck stuck out her tongue at Fanny. "I'd be happy if I weren't your sister," she said. "You make me sick."

"Stop!" ordered Maggie.

But Duck and Fanny would not stop.

"That kind of vulgar impertinence is exactly what I mean," Fanny said, straightening her back and shoulders and standing to her full height. She stared down at Duck with her most withering scowl. "When Mother was about to pass away, she told me she worried about leaving you. She was happy about the other children. She knew she could trust them to behave—to be reasonable, good children. But you, Duck. You are different."

Fanny's words cut into Duck like sharp thorns into bare feet. She could not think what to say. She felt too stunned. Her eyes filled with tears. She turned and ran to the wagon under which Dash was hiding in the shade. She buried her face in the pronghorn's soft neck and sobbed. It was the first time she had cried since Mother died.

Chapter 9

Early the next morning Duck felt something brush against her face. In her half-wakefulness she thought it was Watch. But when she opened her eyes, she realized that it was not her old faithful dog. It was Dash. The pronghorn licked her cheek, which was still salty from her tears the night before. Duck pushed away the little animal and struggled to her feet.

She felt tired and sore and thirsty. Dash butted his head against her arm. "Be patient!" Duck whispered. She crumbled a scrap of stale hardtack from her pocket for the pronghorn to eat. Dash bleated and quickly nibbled every last crumb from her hand. "That's all," Duck said.

Everyone was still asleep. The camp was quiet. Duck walked to the provision wagon. She opened the top of the water cask and was able to scoop out only a small handful of brown water. She took a few sips and then let Dash lick her hand. Hanging from the wagon was Fanny's apron. Seeing that gingham apron made Duck recall every cruel word her sister had said to her the night before.

No one had come to her defense. Not Maggie. Not even Kit or Sonny, who had witnessed what really happened during the Ox Bouncing Game. Everyone was too afraid of Fanny. Discouraged and hopeless, Duck shuffled around the wagon. As she walked, she ran a finger against the wagon's wooden frame. Dash followed close behind her, pulling away whatever wisps of grass he could find on the ground. Duck scowled and thought very hard. There had to be some way to get back at Fanny. So high and mighty and mean.

The blue Dutch plates! If only she could smash each precious plate one by one. That would teach Fanny a lesson. Duck imagined the lovely crashing sound each plate would make when it broke into a million pieces. Fanny would surely regret her words when she found out that Duck had hurtled her marvelous Dutch plates off the side of a cliff.

But how could she get her hands on the plates? They were sewed inside Father's featherbed. Removing them without him—anyone else—noticing would be impossible. Duck paused. Something caught her eye. Ahead, on the corner ledge of the wagon near the driver's seat, she saw something brown. She pulled it out. The journal! Last night Jenny must have forgotten it. She'd be in trouble with Father for leaving the expensive journal out all night.

Duck turned the journal over and over in her hands. The cover was worn and fragile where Jenny held it. Duck opened it. On the back of the inside cover she recognized a few small, silly faces that Maggie must have drawn. Maggie was no artist. She always made people look as though their heads were cider barrels. Maggie was a good speller, though. On occasion she was given the job of writing in the journal. Duck was never allowed this privilege. Father said her penmanship was too awful.

Duck flipped through the pages to the most recent entry:

. . . All owing to want of proper discipline on the part of our youngest herder, Harriet Louise Scott, we were forced to encamp on Marshy creek; the water is poor and after we halted and unyoked our cattle, we discovered a dead horse and ox about 20 steps from our wagons, which caused us all to feel much discontented and for a few moments a bystander would have thought us a grumbling company. I named this spot Camp Desolation.

—Jenny

Want of proper discipline? Duck had only been trying to help find water. Was it her fault there wasn't any? Why, Jenny had blamed the whole campsite disaster on her. She had even used Duck's proper name, Harriet Louise—a name she absolutely despised. Just to make sure everyone would know exactly who was at fault.

Duck slammed the journal shut. One day *everyone* would read what Jenny wrote. Isn't that what she had said? She was going to publish the journal and make Fanny an inspiration for people everywhere—people she had never met. And what about Duck? People would read about how she was the sister responsible for this terrible campsite with a dead ox and a dead horse and no water. She scowled. She wanted to be remembered for being dashing and brave, tall and free — a real cowboy high in the saddle. She did not wish to be remembered for Camp Desolation.

Duck tried to think what to do. She despised both her sisters. Fanny said cruel, hurtful things that made her cry. Jenny used her precious, proud words to cheat and tell lies. Duck wanted to do something that would make Fanny and Jenny howl with regret. But what? Then she had an idea. If she hid the journal, no one would know of Fanny as an inspiration — "wise, unselfish and dedicated to everyone's welfare." No one would read about Camp Desolation. Without this journal, Jenny would never become famous. Instead, she'd be in terrible trouble. Father would punish her severely. Duck's revenge would be complete.

Duck tucked the journal inside her apron and walked quickly out of camp with Dash right behind her. She scanned the rocks for a perfect hiding place. There! She wedged the journal in a crack between two large skull-shaped boulders. No one would ever find it. The journal was as good as destroyed. Duck smiled. "That will show Fanny and Jenny," she said to Dash. Together, they hurried back to camp.

By the time the sun rose, the drivers had yoked the oxen so the caravan could set off again. It was already very hot, even though the sun was only peeking over the horizon. The wagons creaked and groaned like complaining animals as they rocked from side to side along the deeply rutted road. Maggie volunteered to keep an eye on Dash, who followed her slowly.

"Have you seen Jenny's journal anywhere?" Maggie asked as she led the pronghorn away.

"No," lied Duck.

"She told me she's looked everywhere," said Maggie, "and she's scared to death to tell Father it's disappeared."

"Too bad," said Duck, who turned away to hide her grin. She raised one hand to wave good-bye, afraid that if she lingered a moment longer, her sister would guess what she had done.

IN SEARCHING FOR WATER along dry sandy beds of streams, it is well to try the earth with a stick or ramrod, and if this indicates moisture, water will generally be obtained by excavation. Streams often sink in light and porous sand, and sometimes make their appearance again lower down, where the bed is more tenacious; but it is a rule with prairie travelers in searching for water in a sandy country to ascend the streams and the nearer their sources are approached the more water will be found in a dry season.

—THE PRAIRIE TRAVELER

The caravan set off again that morning. In the distance Duck could see new mountains that never seemed to get any closer. She could make out something green in the far distance at the base of the range. Perhaps there would be trees ahead and a cool fresh river. "Get along!" she shouted to two oxen who lowed pathetically. One stumbled to its knees, exhausted and panting for water.

Suddenly the beast lunged forward and fell to the ground with a thud. "John!" Duck shouted. "Come quick! Belle just collapsed."

John MacDonald rode up from behind. He leaned over in his saddle and stared down at the ox with the open eyes. "Poor thing. She's worn out and starved out." He swung down out of his saddle to take a closer look.

"Is she just resting?" Duck asked hopefully.

"No. She's moved on to greener acres," he replied. "I'm afraid she's dead."

Duck stared at the first oxen to die in her care. Belle had walked so far with her. For the first time Duck felt bad about the Ox Bouncing Game. She'd be awfully upset if some children came along later and bounced on Belle the way she and her brothers and sister had with the other ox.

"A terrible waste," John MacDonald said. "If only she'd been able to hold out a little longer."

"You think there's water ahead?" Duck asked.

"That's what everybody's saying," he replied. He climbed back into his saddle. "I'll go tell your father what happened to the ox. You keep your eye on the rest. If we're lucky, they won't all drop before we reach the next spring."

Duck took one last look at the dead ox. She prodded Shuttleback on, who limped and stumbled slower and slower. "Now, don't you give up on me, too," she whispered into the big horse's ear. "Just keep on putting one foot in front of the other. Soon you'll be chest deep in water, so fresh cold it'll make your teeth hurt. And won't that be fine?"

Shuttleback only snorted.

Duck rode behind Mother's Wagon. When she peeked inside, she saw Chat and Wilkie looking holloweyed and sad. "Are we there yet?" Chat asked. "I'm so thirsty I can't even spit."

"Try singing then," Duck said in a bright voice.

"I can't sing, either," Chat complained. "My throat's too dry." Her whine was as shrill as a wagon wheel needing grease.

"We'll reach water in a little while," Duck promised, even though she had no idea how long that would take. Unlike Chat, Wilkie remained silent. He did not complain. The wagon jolted and lurched along, sending the pale boy nearly flying. He clung to a comforter, his mouth a grim line. "Are you all right, Wilkie?" Duck asked.

The little boy nodded, but she knew he was lying.

"Wilkie told me Demon's run away," Chat said.

Duck felt flabbergasted. "How can he know where that cow is when he's inside this wagon?"

Chat shrugged. "Don't you think you better go get her?"

Duck remembered what had happened to Sukey and pulled Shuttleback's reins and turned her horse around. Once again, Wilkie amazed her. He had such an uncanny sense of what was going to happen. She wondered how he knew so much. Desperately, she scanned the cloud of dust for a sign of their precious milk cow. Father would be furious if Demon vanished.

Duck knew the stubborn cow was slow moving. She had a habit of following her nose into the most unlikely places looking for better grass. She'd poisoned herself twice already on alkali-poisoned grass. Fortunately, Uncle Levi worked fast and poured a whole bucket of water mixed with flour down her throat and saved her.

"Demon!" Duck hollered. She wondered how Demon could get away so easily. She searched a cluster of rocks and could not find a sign of the cow. Was it possible the cow had wandered ahead of the caravan? Something must have spurred her into a trot. Only the scent of water could do that, Duck decided.

Duck kicked Shuttleback in the ribs and headed south. She rode on and on, zigzagging back and forth to check behind every clump of sagebrush, every large boulder. In the distance she could see a place where the land suddenly seemed to disappear. Was it a cliff? Nervously she prodded Shuttleback forward. To her amazement, down at the bottom was a hidden grove of shrub willows. She heard the distinctive sound of a cow mooing. Quickly she dismounted and led Shuttleback down the steep place.

She paused. The cow was down there. She was sure. And there was something else singing beyond the trees. Moving water! She and Shuttleback moved through the willows. The horse picked up the fresh scent and plunged faster through the undergrowth. A gleam of reflected sunlight flashed between the trees. Duck licked her lips in anticipation. *Adventures await.* But what if she was only dreaming? What if the precious water were only a mirage?

Shuttleback rushed and stumbled down the steep embankment. As soon as Shuttleback's hooves splashed in the shallow depths, Duck knew something was wrong. The horse backed up and tried to rear. She managed to get one hoof out of the water before she began to sink slowly.

Quicksand!

Chapter

10

Duck dug her heels into the soft embankment. She clutched the reins and held tight. Shuttleback whinnied. What if she were pulled in, too? She yelled at the top of her lungs. "Help! Help!" But who could hear her? The wagon train was a mile away or more. John MacDonald had gone to talk to Father. Her only hope was that another wagon train coming up from behind might hear her and come to her aid. But that might not be for hours and hours. By then it would be too late.

Shuttleback rolled her good eye and whinnied again. The more she struggled, the quicker she seemed to sink. Already her legs had disappeared. The water reached her belly. "Help!" Duck screamed. "Somebody help me!"

No one came. Duck could not let go of the reins. She could not lose this horse. Father would be furious. Her aching hands were sore and blistered now. Her legs were wet. She was so close to water, yet she was unable to drink any. She could not even think about how thirsty she felt. She had to hold on to Shuttleback.

The horse sank deeper and deeper into the water. Now the water was nearly to her shoulder. Her one good eye looked at Duck pleadingly. She made another piteous, piercing whinny.

Suddenly through the willows came a crashing sound. "Hold on!" John MacDonald called.

"Quicksand!" Duck squeaked breathlessly.

"I'll get more help. Don't let go!" John Mac-Donald said. He disappeared as quickly as he had come.

Duck tried to do what he said. She tried not to give up. She talked in a soothing voice to Shuttleback. "You're not going to die, Shuttleback," she whispered. "I'm not going to let you." She held on as tightly as she could, but what good would that do if the quicksand eventually swallowed the horse whole?

"We're coming!" shouted a voice.

She heard the crashing of horses in the willows behind her. Father and three men on horseback plunged a long pole into the water under Shuttleback. A rope was flung out around the horse's neck. Everything happened so fast and so furiously, Duck scarcely knew what was going on. She only worried they were too late. Shuttleback had stopped struggling. She had stopped fighting. Was she dead—just like Belle?

The men rolled a rock on shore, positioning it under the pole to create a kind of lever. All three leaned on the end of the pole. Little by little, the horse was jiggled and lifted. They pried her and pulled her and swore at her. The other horses, attached now with long ropes, pulled Shuttleback downstream. She splashed in the water and finally stumbled out on to dry land, dripping and exhausted.

The men whooped. They filled their hats with water and splashed each other. "Water! Water!" they screamed.

"You did it, Duck," John MacDonald said. "You found us water."

Duck blushed. At last she had done something remarkable—even if finding the water had been an accident. "If you hadn't heard me and gone for help, I would have lost Shuttleback for sure," she told John. "Thanks."

"It's a good thing you got such a big voice for such a little girl," he said. "I heard you yell half a mile away. And you never gave up. I admire that."

Father plowed through the underbrush. He dipped his hand and drank from the river. "Must be a tributary of the Snake," he said. "MacDonald, you rope that cow, lead her home. When you get back, tell the others to bring every cask and barrel to fill with water."

"Yes, sir," John MacDonald replied.

Father splashed water on the back of his neck, soaked his handkerchief, and wiped his face. It was the first time Duck had been alone with Father since they left Illinois. She waited silently, terrified that at any moment she would be punished for nearly losing a horse and the only milk cow they had left. Trembling, she waited. She held the reins as Shuttleback slurped the water up between her teeth. *What will he say? What will he do?*

Father did not speak. He did not look at her. Finally he reached over and, in one swift movement, picked her up and sat her down on Shuttleback's wet, muddy saddle. He gave the tired old horse a slap. "Now, go on!"

That was all.

Stunned, Duck rode along until she caught up with John, who led Demon with a rope. He grinned and doffed his hat, making a formal little flourishing bow. "Well done!" he said. "The milk cow's safe and sound and water's been located. Good work!"

Duck tried to smile. Somehow she couldn't. She felt so confused. She had expected to be punished by Father. She had assumed he'd be angry for the way she had almost lost Demon and Shuttleback. Somehow she believed he knew every other awful thing she'd ever done as well—including hiding the journal. Without meaning to, Duck suddenly burst into tears. Once she started, she couldn't stop.

John looked at her in alarm. "What's wrong?" he asked. "Are you hurt?"

Duck shook her head. "I'm not good," she said, sobbing. "I'm not reasonable. I'm different. That's why my mother worried when she died. She said she worried about leaving me. She couldn't ever trust me to behave."

"Who told you that?"

"Fanny."

John pulled out a dusty red handkerchief from his pocket. "Here," he said. "Use this."

She blew her nose loudly. For a few minutes he did not say anything. "Don't cry, little girl. If you were the naughtiest, you can bet your mother loved you a tiny bit the best. That's the way mothers are."

Duck took a deep breath. Mother loved her best. But somehow she still didn't feel very happy. *To do what is right, no matter how hard.* She thought and thought. What would Mother want her to do so that she wouldn't feel so awful? Finally she had an idea. *The journal.*

FRESH TRACKS generally show moisture where the earth has been turned up, but often in short exposure to the sun they become dry. If the tracks be very recent, the sand may sometimes, where it is very loose and dry, be seen running back into the tracks, and by following them to a place where they cross water, the earth will be wet for some distance after they leave it. . . . It is very easy to tell whether tracks have been made before or after a rain as the water washes off the sharp edges.

—THE PRAIRIE TRAVELER

The next morning very early before anyone awoke, Duck saddled Shuttleback and headed up the road, following the route they'd taken the day before—the way back to Marsh Creek and Camp Desolation. She urged Shuttleback on as quickly as the horse could carry her. Once her family and the hired men awoke, the caravan would be on its way again. Someone would notice she was missing.

It was barely four miles back to Marsh Creek. She knew she was getting close as the smell became stronger. How much time would she have to find the journal and return unnoticed? She scanned the rocks, trying to remember the exact spot where they had camped the night before. Wilkie was right. Every campsite looked like every other campsite since they'd left Fort Laramie.

A cloud of dust coming over the horizon warned Duck that in less than an hour another group of travelers on their way west would be coming this way. Anxiously she surveyed the rocks. She pulled on the reins to stop Shuttleback. *Is this the spot?* She thought she remembered the stones that Sonny had piled in a circle. But there were so many other fire rings, so many other beaten-down places along the road that had served as places for tired families to spend the night. *How can I be sure?*

Desperately she rode up and down the road, backward and forward, trying to remember. Was this the place? Or that? Any moment the wagons would roll past and the dust would block her view and confuse her even more. She turned Shuttleback off the road and wandered among the large boulders. Finding the journal seemed hopeless. She wished she had never hidden it. The journal was as good as destroyed now. There was no way she'd locate it.

Duck circled around a cluster of boulders farther south from the road. Suddenly she spotted something out of the corner of her eye. She urged Shuttleback closer. As she did, the horse suddenly whinnied and flattened her ears against her head.

"What's the matter?" Duck said, frightened. *What if it's an Indian hiding? What if it's Critchfield?* She recalled his angry, hateful stare when he left the caravan. Duck pulled Shuttleback to a halt. The mare minced sideways, then reared. Duck clung to the mane. When Shuttleback rocked forward again, Duck slipped from the saddle to the ground. Holding the reins, she walked boldly toward the spot. She wasn't going to let Critchfield scare her off.

"Come out here, you trifling fool!" she shouted, using John's phrase. *You must seek them out and see them through doing what is right, no matter how hard.*

"Fool! Fool!" her echo answered.

Duck's legs shook. *Maybe I should give up.* But if she galloped back to camp, she knew she'd never find the courage to return again. The journal would be gone for good. In a little while the sun would be up. She didn't have much time.

Think. Think. She closed her eyes. *Skull-shaped boulders.* She opened her eyes. Something fluttered. She twisted in time to see pages flap open in the wind. The journal! She ran to the spot and turned the journal over and over to make sure it was all in one piece. Nothing had changed. The journal looked exactly as it had when she hid it between the rocks.

She scanned the sky. The sun would rise soon. She didn't have much time to get back. So that the journal wouldn't be lost again, she tucked it inside her belt. She quickly mounted Shuttleback and turned the big horse west again. In the distance she could hear the sound of creaking wagons coming down the hill.

"Hallo, gal!" someone shouted.

Duck waved.

"Any idea how far to a good spring? Something smells foul here," the driver called. He was an elderly man with a gray beard. His gaunt-faced children peeked out from behind the dirty canvas wagon top.

"It's four miles to the next creek where there's tolerable good grass," Duck said.

"You're awfully brave to be traveling alone," he said. "T'isn't safe."

Duck smiled. She sat up straight in the saddle and hoped she looked brave and bold. "I'm on my way to meet my family ahead," she said and waved. She didn't want to have to explain to anyone what she was doing prowling around an empty campsite. Along the way to Oregon, strangers had a way of meeting up with one another again and again. It wasn't far-fetched to think that Father might have a conversation with this man.

Hurriedly Duck prodded Shuttleback into a

trot. The horse ambled along at a rolling pace. Duck scanned the ruts ahead. She rode and rode. Finally she recognized a familiar sound— Chat singing. *The campsite!*

To her intense relief, no one looked surprised to see her when she arrived. They were too busy loading casks of water into the wagons. Even Harvey looked like a changed person. His hair was back to its normal brown color. The green tinge around his nose and ears was gone. "Where you been on Old Crowbait?" he demanded when he saw Duck and Shuttleback.

"She's not Old Crowbait. She's a good horse," she said with a superior sniff and patted muddy Shuttleback. "We've been out looking for strays." She hoped her brother wouldn't notice she was lying or that she had a bulky square object hidden inside her skirt. "What's that commotion going on in the wagon? Somebody in an argument with Father?"

Harvey shook his head. "More likely it's Father doing all the arguing. He's scolding String Bean. Seems she can't find the journal to write about what happens today." He shook his head in mock sorrow. "I'm glad I'm not her. If that journal's lost, she'll be skinned alive."

Chapter

11

Duck's legs ached as she slid off the saddle. In one arm she clutched the journal hidden in a fold of her apron. She struggled with her free hand to grab Shuttleback's reins and pull the horse toward the area where the cattle were grazing.

Her brother shook his head in disgust. "You got off that horse just like a girl," he said in a scornful voice.

Duck smiled at her brother as sweetly as she could. She didn't want to pick a fight with him now—not when she was on an important mission. She had to find a way to hide the journal again without anyone's noticing what she was doing. Near one of the barrels she saw her chance. She sidled up behind it and carefully slipped the journal on top of the lid. She made sure the journal wouldn't fall inside the barrel. As naturally as possible, she brushed her hands and ambled toward the campfire where Kit was packing up tinware.

"Duck!" whispered Kit. "Have you seen the journal? Father's in a rage. We've looked everywhere."

Duck hoped she looked genuinely puzzled. "Why not try that water barrel? I just saw something odd over there."

Kit ran to the barrel. She whooped.

Duck smiled. She felt happy—even though there was no way to explain her happiness. Kit skipped across the camp to tearful Jenny. Duck couldn't hear their voices, but she could see Jenny suddenly embrace her sister. Now she was smiling, too. Father shook his finger at the two girls. He took the journal and flipped through the pages as if to check if everything was all right. Seemingly satisfied, he handed the journal back to Jenny. Duck knew, even so far away that she couldn't hear a word, that Father was warning her never to leave the journal out of her sight. Duck knew she never would again.

Maggie hurried to Duck carrying a pail of water. "Isn't it wonderful?" she said breathlessly. "The journal's safe."

Duck nodded. She didn't want to talk too much about what had happened for fear that the expression on her face would give her away. "Are you taking the water to Dash?" she asked Maggie.

Maggie bit her lip. She put the pail on the ground.

"What's the matter?" Duck demanded. "What happened to Dash?"

"He's gone," Maggie mumbled. "I was going to tell you. I just didn't know how."

"What do you mean he's gone?" Duck asked anxiously. "When I left him early this morning, he seemed all right. What are you talking about?"

"He didn't die," Maggie said quickly. "It was Father who let him go just a few hours ago. He said there wasn't enough food to keep a pet. The pronghorn took off like a shot for the hills."

Duck felt too stunned to speak. "Dash was mine," she said finally. "He was so little. So helpless. He'll never survive out there alone."

"I'm sorry," Maggie said.

"Why didn't you do something? Why didn't you refuse to give him up?" Duck demanded. "You worked as hard as I did to keep Dash alive."

Maggie shrugged. "I'm not like you. I can't go against Father."

Angrily Duck kicked the precious pail of water as hard as she could. The water splashed all over Maggie's skirt. She raced away, crying. Duck didn't feel any better. Now her foot hurt. She stomped to the wagon where Dash used to sleep and climbed under it. *How could Maggie do this to her?*

"Do you want some breakfast, Duck?" Fanny called.

"No!" Duck shouted. She wrapped a burlap sack around her shoulders and cried so softly that no one could hear. Even so, each time she shut her eyes, the big soft eyes of the pronghorn still haunted her.

❧

To Mary Augusta Brown

Dear Cousin

Although we are far separated and I may never again behold your face yet you ever remain as deer to me as when i enjoyed you company daily I hope that you got my letter that Father left at Fort Boyse with many others We have but little time to devote to writing having so much work to do I am sorry to tell you that old Flower died on Snake river she did not tare our dresses any on the road as she used to in the pasture Do you remember when we went to visit her? She enjoyed our songs so much even tho they was very loud We have got a cow that is a great deal like her she cost seventy-six dollars but she is not such a good looking cow as old flower was old Suckey got drowned in the river we lost a lot a great deal of our property on the road Ther is some places on the road that is impossible to travel The weather is verry warm we have to travel 15 miles & upwards without water when we get to it it

is not like the water at home but so warm
that we can hardly drink it 600 miles since
Fort Hall there is nothing to be seen but
sand dust & sage plains Now I have lost
my mother and I have lost my pronghorn
whose name was Dash and was an orphan
My heart feels as if it mite break Maggie
says she is sorry Dash is gone but I am
thinking that there is another on this wagon
trane that she would miss more if he was
to run off for the hills like that poorr little
pronghorn If you see old Watch will you
give him special loving care for me?
please write to me in Oregon territory
　　　yours truly
　　　　H.M.S. (Duck)

❧

. . . *Wagons push on 300 miles through some of
the hardest country yet. We follow the perilous Snake
River, winding up and down steep canyon walls. In
many places chained wheels aren't enough to keep the
wagons from rolling too fast. The poor exhausted oxen
have to walk behind the wagons and lower the loads*

slowly down the steep hills. The Snake roils and curls around the rocks below us. Twice we have to ford. During one dangerous crossing, five oxen and one horse drowned—swept downriver. After that, the wild current booms and crashes even in my dreams.

—Jenny

The wagon track was rocky, dusty, and hot. Whatever grass there was had been picked clean by other wagon teams that had gone ahead. There were no trees, no shade. Duck's shoes were nearly gone. Every day she strapped the few pieces of leather left around her feet and tried as best she could to avoid the stinging prickly pear. In some places she had to wade through knee-deep dust as thick as snow. The fine dust was stirred up easily. It floated in such a great cloud, she could barely see the wagon ahead of her as she climbed up and up. The old horse wheezed so badly after a tough climb, Duck wondered if the mare would make it to Oregon.

Most alarming was the way that the wagons began to fall to pieces. The wood dried out and the axles cracked. Axles and wheels had to be replaced and repaired and replaced again. The teams that pulled the heavy wagons soon gave out under the strain. Bally and Buck, Poullup and Popcorn, Bright and Berry, Belle and Butter were gone. As the oxen died along the roadside, there were none to replace them.

Other travelers had suffered from the same fate. The roadside was littered with cast-off broken wagons, dead oxen, too-heavy furniture and broken barrels and casks. Duck and her brothers found a fancy wicker baby carriage with no wheels, a heavy set of leather-bound books, a doll with no head, fancy hair pins, a heavy gilded mirror nearly cracked to pieces and a dirty hair brush with a broken handle. They searched abandoned barrels and boxes for food. But there never was any. Someone else had been here first to scavenge. Food was precious. The next real settlement was the Dalles. Until they reached this small town in Oregon Territory, flour, salt pork, and coffee could only be bought at high, outlandish prices from other passing travelers.

August 14

We started this morning in good season as we had

16 miles to go and 14 of the last without grass or water we found this the hardest day on our teams of any yet traveled, we arrived late in evening thirsty & weary with poor grass for our cattle; here we lost another of our cattle from drinking too much water This makes eight head we have lost out of our five teams which makes them rather light and in all probability we will have to leave one of our wagons.

—Maggie

The next morning Father announced that they would have to abandon Mother's Wagon. "We don't have any choice," he said. "There's not enough oxen to pull all five wagons anymore."

Chat and Wilkie were moved into the Salon Wagon. Duck and her sisters unloaded blankets and comforters. Some bedding had to be left behind. The hired men pulled the wheels from the wagon to use later as replacements.

The last direct connection with Mother—gone. "It's so sad, isn't it?" Duck said to Maggie, who stood watching the wagon slowly being dismantled. She shot a quick glance at her sister. As usual, Maggie wasn't listening. She gazed off into space. *She's thinking about John MacDonald again, I bet.* As far as Duck was concerned, her sister already spent far too much time with John. She ate meals seated beside him. She mended his shirts. She chatted and joked with him whenever she could. *I might as well be invisible.* Duck sighed loudly.

"What did you say?" Maggie said.

"Losing Mother's Wagon," Duck replied. "It's too bad, isn't it?"

Maggie looked at Duck. Her eyes were red and puffy. "I can think of a lot sadder things to lose than a dumb wagon."

Now what's the matter? Duck watched in astonishment as her sister stomped away. Only later that morning did Duck hear the news. John MacDonald and four other hired men were leaving.

"We'll buy the wagon bed from you," John told Father. "We're going to caulk the seams and float it downriver to the Dalles. I'm sorry to leave you, but the boys are anxious to get to Oregon. They figure river travel's faster than driving behind oxen."

Father did not look pleased. "What will you do when you come to the rapids in your home-made boat?"

"Pray hard," John replied.

"I guess I have no choice but to let you go and wish you luck," Father said. They shook hands.

The next day when John and the others prepared to leave, Maggie was so inconsolable, Duck worried she might be ill. Duck spied on her sisters behind one of the wagons.

"I can't believe he's going," Maggie sobbed on Jenny's shoulder.

"There, there," Jenny said. Then added angrily, "It's a mystery to me how he can desert us like this."

Maggie sobbed louder.

"Is there anything I can do?" Duck asked, stepping out from behind the wagon.

"No, go away," her sisters replied.

Duck slunk out of sight again. She felt sad to see John go, too. He had been kind to her. He had given her the pronghorn. He had helped her and Shuttleback in the quicksand. He was a good listener and he knew how to keep a secret. All the same, she wondered if things would be better after he left. *Maybe Maggie will be my friend again.*

The next morning John and the four others

hauled their few belongings aboard the caulked wagon box. Duck stood sadly with her sisters on the shore. Maggie wept openly.

John tipped his hat. "Goodbye!" he said to Duck and her sisters.

"Good luck!" Duck replied, surprised to find herself wiping tears from her eyes.

Maggie blew her nose loudly. "Don't go!" she cried.

"We're running out of supplies and time," John said. "We'll get to Oregon faster this way and be less of a burden to your father. In a day or two he won't be able to feed us."

Maggie sniffled. "Floating by boat's dangerous. Be careful."

"We will," John MacDonald promised. He shook hands with Sonny and Harvey. Then he helped the other hired men push the boat into the shallow water. One by one they waded out and climbed aboard. Between the five of them, they had three long poles to navigate.

At first the wagon-box boat trembled in the water. Would it sink? The boat turned, caught the current, and began to move. It turned one way, then the other.

"She doesn't know her bow from her stern," Father called.

When the boat righted itself and headed downstream, the men cheered.

"Sure beats walking and eating dust!" one shouted.

"See you in Oregon!" another called and waved his hat.

"Yippeeaoh!" called Harvey and Sonny.

"Yippeeaoh!" Chat echoed.

"Do you think we'll ever see them again?" Fanny asked.

"I don't know," Kit replied quietly.

Maggie did not say anything. She and Duck stood and peered down the river until the little boat was out of sight. Fanny walked with Chat, Kit, and Jenny back to the campsite. Harvey and Sonny went to collect wood.

"Maggie, want something to eat?" Duck asked. She took from her pocket a small tough piece of gray biscuit. "Maybe this will cheer you. You can have this. I can't hardly chew it anyhow. My mouth's too sore."

"I'll never eat again," Maggie said dramatically and shuffled away.

Confused and hurt, Duck watched her sister

go. *What if she only acts worse now that he's gone?* Duck's heart felt very hollow. She glanced down the river one more time. John and Mother's Wagon were gone, and she knew neither was ever coming back.

August 19

We came nine very hilly miles and finding some dry bunch grass we encamped to rest our stock and let them graze Our cattle are very much jaded and manny of them too worn out to work; A number of the company and two in our family is sick; some in other wagon trains nearby dangerously ill; in consequence we feel much discouraged. We are encamped upon the river bank . . . the afternoon is very cold light showers are falling at intervals and the western wind is quite strong. We are all very tired as each person has to walk who is able to go alone

—Jenny

Ahead loomed the Cascade Mountains covered with snow. Duck wondered what they would do when they reached those cold heights without enough warm clothes and scarcely any shoes between them. What worried her most was their dwindling food supply. The salt pork was gone. The flour barrel was almost empty. How long could so little nourishing food keep them alive, especially now that Wilkie and Chat had taken a turn for the worse?

That morning the ground had been covered with frost. Although it was still August, she could smell winter on the way. She saddled Shuttleback but walked beside the horse all morning to spare the mare the extra effort of carrying her. Duck put one foot ahead of the other and walked without thinking. When the wagon train came to a spring, the water was warm and muddy and smelled of sulphur. They kept moving on.

Finally the road turned away from the Snake River. The country changed. The hills lay covered with thick green grass. Shuttleback lingered every few steps to eat, as if worried that there wouldn't be any more ahead. The oxen stood up to their bellies in thick grass. The caravan stopped and camped early that day to let the oxen eat their fill.

Duck lay in the grass and stared up at the cloud-filled sky. She thought about Mother. *I hope there's plenty of food in heaven.*

"Too bad we can't eat grass like the buffalo. That's one thing there's plenty of here," Harvey announced. He stood over her with an armful of buffalo chips, dried buffalo dung that was used as fuel for their cooking fire. "Want to have a buffalo chip-throwing contest?"

Duck shook her head. She didn't have the energy.

"You're no fun," Harvey said. He looked into the distance to the west. "See that ribbon of water? They call it the Burnt River, Father said. That's a strange name for it, don't you think? Don't look like it was on fire to me."

Duck sat up and leaned on one elbow. She shielded her eyes and looked out in the direction Harvey was pointing. Beyond she could see a range of mountains. As the sun began to set, she noticed how the mountains caught the light and seemed to glow. "That range over there's pretty red," Duck said. She picked a tender piece of grass and chewed the end. "They look like they're burning. Maybe that's how the river got the name."

"Duck!" Kit shouted from the back of the Salon Wagon.

"What do you want?" Duck said.

"Come in here and watch Chat and Wilkie for me," Kit said. "They're asking for you. I haven't hardly had a minute of peace from them all day."

Duck sighed. She spit the grass from her mouth. "Got to go," she told Harvey.

"Think fast," Harvey said. He flipped her a buffalo chip. She caught it as it sailed through the air. "Nice catch," he said, grinning.

Duck absentmindedly threw and caught the buffalo chip as she approached the wagon. "Why do you got to holler so loud?" she complained to Kit.

"You'd holler loud, too, if you was trapped in a wagon all day with two sick children," Kit complained. "I need some fresh air." She jumped to the ground. "And don't bring that filthy thing inside."

Duck made a face. Since her bossy sister didn't want her to bring the buffalo chip inside, that was exactly what she'd do.

"Hello, Duck! Play with us," Chat commanded. Her round face was thinner now and sallow colored. Like her brother, she had been sick to her stomach for the past thirty miles. But she continued to wear the little silver thimble on one finger that Grandfather had given her to take on the trip. She refused to take it off. She claimed it was magic.

Wilkie seemed to be worse. Something about bad water, Father said. But what else was there to drink?

"How are you, Wilkie?" Duck asked.

Her brother smiled faintly. His face was thin. There were dark circles beneath his eyes. The wagon smelled sour. Duck rolled up the flaps to let in more air.

"What did you bring?" Chat demanded.

Duck looked down at the buffalo chip. "A piano."

"A piano?" Chat frowned. "Looks like an old dry cow pie to me."

"You have to use your imagination," Duck said. "Right, Wilkie?" Wilkie seemed to perk up a little. Encouraged, Duck continued. "Now, listen real carefully and you'll hear music."

Chat clapped her little hands together. "I love music. Just like at church. Remember that music at church, Duck? They played it so loud. Everybody sings. I can sing. Do you want to hear me sing?"

Duck put her finger to her mouth to hush her sister. Now she understood why Kit wanted to escape. Chat talked too much. "You can't talk while I play," she told her sister. "You have to listen so you hear the music." Duck shook her fingers. Then she moved them up and down the buffalo chip with a flourish.

"Oh, it's so beautiful!" Chat said. "Can you hear it, Wilkie?"

Wilkie smiled and nodded.

"What song do you want me to play next?" Duck asked.

"Something happy. A happy song. Can I hum along?" Chat asked.

Duck nodded. She played the pretend piano and Chat sang. They performed a dozen duets. "Now let's do something else," Duck said.

"What?" demanded Chat. "I liked that music. Play some more."

"No. Let Wilkie decide. What do you want to do now, Wilkie?"

"Don't ask Wilkie," Chat begged. "All he wants to do is talk about sad things."

"What sad things?" Duck asked, trying not to appear alarmed.

"He talks about how he wants to go to heaven so he can see Mother," Chat said and frowned. "Don't you, Wilkie?"

For the first time Wilkie spoke. "Horse and wagon," he whispered weakly.

"He wants to play horse and wagon," Duck said. "See? That's a fun game."

Chat looked disappointed. "I don't like that game."

"It's Wilkie's choice," Duck said. "I'm going to show you a new way to play. Where's the sewing basket?"

"Over there," said Chat, still pouting. She took the thimble off and tried it on each finger one by one. "That was Mother's, wasn't it? Do you miss Mother? I want my mother." Pretty soon, Chat was crying.

"Don't cry," Duck hissed anxiously. She looked over at Wilkie, worried that he'd burst into tears, too. And then what would she do? Quickly Duck dumped out the contents of the sewing basket and found four spools of thread. "I need you to help me, Chat. Find some string."

Chat busily searched the wagon. She soon became so intent on finding string, she forgot about crying. "Here!" she said brightly. She handed Duck a small section of rope that had once tied together two comforters.

"Good," Duck replied. She unraveled four

small pieces from the rope. Then she attached the four spools to make wheels for the basket, which had become a wagon. "Now help me find four strong beetles."

"I won't touch bugs," Chat said using a ladylike grimace she had obviously copied from Fanny.

Duck rolled her eyes. She quickly caught four black shining beetles that crawled beneath the wagon. She climbed back inside carrying the beetles trapped inside her pocket, which she held tightly closed at the top. One by one, she took out each beetle and tied a little bit of string around it like a harness. "How do you like our fine prancing horses, Wilkie?" she asked.

Wilkie watched with great interest as the four beetles with strings attached struggled to pull the wagon across the floor. Chat clapped with delight. The wagon went on many trips. Soon the two children drifted off to sleep. Chat curled up in one corner with her finger in her mouth. Wilkie slept on his side with a quilt wrapped around him. Every so often his face twitched as if he were having a bad dream.

Duck freed the exhausted beetles. Then she tiptoed to the end of the wagon and leaped to the ground.

Chapter 12

The next dawn was cold and misty. Duck, who was sleeping curled up in the camp equipment wagon, sat up as soon as she heard a loud shout coming from outside. What was happening? An Indian attack? She unwrapped herself from the comforter and peered out from under the wagon canvas. Someone ran past. She crawled out of the wagon and crept toward the voices coming from the Salon Wagon. She could see Fanny and Jenny with their backs toward her. She saw the four remaining hired men with their hats off. Uncle Levi had his hat off, too. He stood beside the wagon tongue, staring down at someone. Duck pushed through the crowd, wondering what had happened.

Then she saw him. Her father sat on the wagon tongue, his shoulders hunched forward, his face in his hands. Then she knew what had happened. Something awful. "It's Wilkie, isn't it?" she whispered to Jenny, who was crying great gulping sobs.

Her sister nodded. "He's gone. The treasure of our hearts."

"Gone?" Duck said, stunned. She had just played with him the day before. He had been sick before and he always recovered. How could he be gone?

"He passed away last night," Jenny said, finally regaining her composure. "Two months and seven days after Mother. At least he isn't suffering anymore."

Mother. Dash and John MacDonald. Now Wilkie. All gone. Numb, Duck turned. She stumbled away from the wagons. For the next hour she threw rocks at a distant boulder and did not speak to anyone.

August 28

Two months and seven days this morning since our beloved mother was called to bid this world adieu, the ruthless monster death not yet content has once more entered our fold & taken in his icy grip the treasure of our hearts! Wilkie is to be buried upon an elevated point 150 feet above the plains in a spot of sweet seclusion.

—Jenny

All through the day and the next night came the ringing sound of pickaxes biting into solid rock. Father ordered that the hired men cut a cavity out of the solid rock that jutted from the top of Burnt River Mountain. The following morning Wilkie was buried there beneath the only other living thing: a little juniper tree.

After the burial everyone came back to camp stunned or weeping. "I can't believe it," Harvey said, blowing his nose on his dirty sleeve. "He seemed to be getting better."

Chat was inconsolable. She and Wilkie had traveled together since the trip began. "How can he be dead?" she said over and over. Kit tried to console her, but Chat pushed her away. "Leave me alone," she said. "I hate you."

Duck sighed. She knew Chat didn't mean it. But there seemed no one who had the energy to remind her of that fact. They were all too tired and worn down. Duck wandered to a rock beside one of the wagons. There she saw Jenny and Maggie sitting together.

"Come here, Duck," Maggie called. "I want you to hear something."

Duck shuffled closer, not really wanting to talk to anyone or hear anything.

"Jenny's written a poem. Read it, won't you?" Maggie asked.

Jenny unfolded the piece of paper in her lap and read aloud:

"Far away over deserts and mountains so wild
In our wearisome journey we've strayed
Towards a far distant land, a bright home in
    the West
Where many fond hopes have been laid.

"The journey has been one of anguish and woe
Combined with some gladness and mirth
Yet we little thought when we started to go
That our hopes would lie low in the earth!

"Some ten weeks ago our dear Mother was
    called
To bid her dear children farewell,

*And Wilkie will meet her beyond yon bright
    stars,
And together in heaven they'll dwell.''*

"Isn't that beautiful?" Maggie asked.

Duck nodded, even though she didn't like poems. They always sounded so fussy. "How come you didn't mention about Wilkie's agreeable manners? And what about his kindness and how smart he was?" she demanded. "You should put that in there somewhere if you're going to make it into a book."

"It's just a beginning," Jenny said in a hurt voice.

"Well, you are going to publish it, aren't you?" Duck asked.

"Certainly," Jenny said.

Duck frowned. Her sister was showing off again. Her precious words! How could she prance around about her writing at a time like this? "Sometimes," Duck said to Jenny, "I think the only person you care about is yourself. And the only thing you care about is one day you'll be famous."

"That's not true!" Jenny replied hotly. "I care about a lot of things. I care about everyone in this family. What about you? You didn't even shed one tear at the funerals for Mother or Wilkie. The only time I saw you cry was when John MacDonald left."

Duck leaped up to grab her sister. She wanted to choke her. Jenny screamed.

"Stop!" said Maggie. She pulled Duck away. "I can't stand it. Come and help find something to eat. Where's Father?"

Duck knew exactly what Maggie was doing. She was trying to change the subject. But Duck would not be stopped.

Jenny glowered at Duck and straightened her dress. Then she pointed to the mountain. "He's still up there."

"When's he coming down?" Maggie asked. She shot a nervous glance at Duck as if she were a firecracker about to explode.

"How should I know?" Duck said, still furious. "He never slowed down one minute when Wilkie was sick. Seems kind of odd he's slowed down and won't move on now that Wilkie's gone."

"That's a horrible thing to say," Jenny said.

"It's the truth," Duck replied. "We never should have left for Oregon. Not with Mother and Wilkie so sick. We never should have come to that 'bright home in the West' you write about. It's all a pack of lies."

Jenny burst into tears.

"You apologize to your sister," Maggie said, her voice quavering with emotion.

"I won't," Duck declared. "I'm telling the truth. You can cry all you want, Jenny." Duck stomped away.

"You don't mean those horrible words," Maggie called after her.

Duck did not stop. She kept walking. Up the hill toward Wilkie's grave. When she got there, she was surprised to see Father. He didn't see her. He sat on a rock staring at the knife in his hand. Every so often he wiped his face with his sleeve. Then she realized. Father was sobbing. Duck didn't know what to do. She had never seen her father cry in all her life. She looked away, embarrassed.

Suddenly all her anger was gone. She peeked at her father again. He looked so broken-down and old sitting there on the rock. He wasn't tall and straight and commanding anymore. He seemed confused and disheveled, like someone who didn't know what he was doing or where he was going. Was he feeling as sad and lost as she was?

Behind him she could just make out carving

on the little juniper tree. So that was what he'd been doing with the knife. He was carving something on the tree. Duck crept closer, still under cover of rocks. When she peeked around, she could just make out what had been freshly carved into the bark. One word.

"Wilkie."

On approaching strangers, Indians put their horses at full speed and persons not familiar with their peculiarities and habits might interpret this as an act of hostility; but it is their custom with friends as well as enemies, and should not occasion groundless alarm . . . all that is necessary to ascertain their disposition is to raise the right hand with the palm in front, and gradually push it forward and back several times. They all understand this to be a command to halt and if they are not hostile it will at once be obeyed . . . After they have stopped the right hand is raised again as before and slowly moved to the right and left, which signifies, "I do not know you. Who are you?"

—The Prairie Traveler

The next morning ice formed in the buckets under the wagons. Duck could see her breath. She shivered as she crawled out of her bed and rolled up the comforter.

"Hurry up," Fanny called. "I need more wood to get this fire going."

Duck, Sonny, and Harvey dragged branches of balsam, alder, and birch that they found along a stream up to the campsite.

"Where's Father?" Duck asked.

"Dunno," Harvey replied.

"He didn't come back last night," Sonny said. "He stayed up there on the mountain all night. I waited for him to come back, but he never did. What if something happens to him?"

"What are you talking about?" Harvey demanded. He piled another branch into the pile.

"What if something happens to Father?" Sonny said in an urgent voice. "Then we'll be orphans. Did you ever think of that?"

Harvey shoved Sonny hard in the shoulder. "Shut up. Nothing's going to happen to Father. He's the toughest person I know."

Duck did not say anything. She thought about what she had seen on the mountain the day before. Father weeping. It was a side of him she had never seen before. And suddenly she felt very worried. If Father lost his spirit, his drive, they'd never make it to Oregon. They'd all perish in these cold, snowy mountains with nothing to eat, no place warm to sleep. She decided not to tell her brothers her worries. They looked anxious enough.

"Hurry up," she scolded them. "You're as slow as turtles. Uncle Levi says we've got to get going. It's going to be snowing soon in the mountains. We won't make it across if we don't hurry."

Eventually Father did return. He spoke to no one. Stone-faced, he climbed into one of the wagons and fell asleep. The caravan traveled fourteen miles that day.

. . . *The rest of the week the road followed the Burnt River, a small stream with a cold, swift current. The weather turned bitter and windy. Beyond the Burnt River, we passed through bluffs and rocky plains and on September 2 to a brow of mountains overlooking the Grand Round River—the worst climb yet. The rutted road clung to the side of a cliff and headed straight up. The rocks so filled the road that anyone who had not begun to 'see the elephant' would have been afraid to have attempt it with heavy wagons and weakened oxen. . . .*

—Jenny

Duck did not know if she and Shuttleback would make it to the summit. The horse stumbled and nearly slipped off the cliff's edge. Dust hid the wagons and rocky road ahead. When fresh wind blew, Duck was able to see for a moment over the edge. The sight of sharp rocks and pounding water far below made her dizzy.

"We can't go any farther," Maggie called. She stood on the trail ahead with Chat, who was crying into her sister's skirt.

"Come on now!" Duck urged. "Shuttleback will help us." She took Chat by the hand and with the horse leading the way, the three girls climbed and climbed. When they reached the top, they had to make the harrowing journey down, which was worst of all.

"I can't," Chat whimpered.

"It's too far," Maggie said. "We'll fall and be killed."

"Don't look down," Duck said. "Just keep your eyes on your feet." She tied Shuttleback's reins loosely to the saddle so that the horse could make her way first, unhindered. Duck smiled at Maggie and Chat as bravely as she could. "Good luck," she told Shuttleback and hoped the tired, old horse would be able to find her way with only one good eye to watch for rocks and holes in the steep road.

The wagons with their wheels chained creaked and groaned down the incline. The oxen strained. Any moment Duck expected to see wagons and teams hurtle over the edge. But somehow they descended, slowly but surely to the Grand Round River below.

September 3

We came, I think 11 miles over the mountains. The scenery was delightful all day but the road was extremely hilly and rough. We halted and prepared our dinner and took a long rest as our cattle were very tired in consequence of the very hard roads of the morning's travel. We then started over the mountains again and traveled three miles, when we came near an excellent spring and encamped having traveled through heavy timber almost all day This is the first night we have camped in heavy trees since we left St. Joe, Missouri. A curious place. Sounds echo and reverberate

from hill to hill to such a degree that the noise of discharging a rifle is equal to the report of a cannon.
—*Maggie*

Duck marveled at the tall, thick stands of yellow pine and balsam fir. The sweet smell of pines! She entered the forest, closed her eyes, and remembered the wood lot on Grandfather's farm. Suddenly she felt very homesick again.

"Ya-hooooo!" someone shouted.

"Ya-hooo! Hooo! Hooo!" came the echo.

"That you, Harvey?" she called.

"Did you hear me?" he said proudly. "Here, have some berries. I found them up on the hill. How'd you like my war whoop?"

Duck ate some of the bitter berries. "The Blue Mountains echo just fine," she said. "I only hope some Indians didn't hear you and come running here for a war party."

"You think so?" Harvey asked, looking nervously over his shoulder. "You couldn't see them in here if they came, could you?"

Duck looked around. After nearly four months on the plains and desert, she had forgotten the penned-in feeling of a real forest. It was dark in here and spooky, and she couldn't see

155 ～♥

very far. Out on the plains where the sky stretched forever, she could see anybody coming. She could spot storms before they hit. All at once, the woods made her nervous. "We'd better get back to camp," she said. "I told Fanny I'd help her with dinner."

"There's not much to cook," Harvey said. "She's making flour gravy again, and she's going to call it flour soup. You hungry?"

Duck nodded.

"Me, too," said Harvey. "When we get to Oregon, I'm going to eat a whole gooseberry pie and four slabs of some good red meat and a pile of mashed potatoes whipped fine. What are you going to eat?"

"Fried eggs, boiled eggs, scrambled eggs with plenty of butter," she said dreamily. "A tower of pancakes a foot high, a rasher of bacon, and fine white bread toast smeared thick with current jelly." The entire walk back to camp, she and her brother talked of nothing but food.

. . . WE HAD NO SALT, sugar, coffee, or tobacco, which, at a time when men are performing the severest labor that a human system is capable of enduring, was a great privation. In this destitute condition we found a substitute for tobacco in the bark of the red willow, which grows upon many of the mountain streams . . . The outer bark is first removed with a knife, after which the inner bark is scraped up into ridges around the sticks and held in the fire until it is thoroughly roasted, when it is taken off the stick, pulverized in the hand, and is ready for smoking . . . a decoction of the dried wild or horse mint, which we found under the snow, was quite palatable, and answered instead of coffee . . . We suffered greatly for want of salt; but by burning the outside of our mule steaks, and sprinkling a little gunpowder on them, it did not require a very extensive stretch of the imagination to fancy the presence of salt and pepper.

—THE PRAIRIE TRAVELER

Chapter

13

Fanny stood over the fire mixing what was left of the mealy flour and some water in a pan. "Have you seen Kit or Jenny?" she asked Duck. "They were supposed to bring more water. It was their turn."

Duck shrugged. She dumped the wood on the ground. "I haven't seen either of them since this morning when we left."

"Well, go and find them for me," Fanny commanded.

Duck looked around the camp. She asked Chat.

"I don't know where they gone," Chat replied. "Hiding maybe?"

She asked Sonny and Harvey.

"Maybe Indians got them," Harvey said.

"Yeah. Maybe they're kidnapped," Sonny said and laughed.

Duck asked Maggie, who sat on a stump writing yet another letter to John MacDonald. *Her hundredth at least.*

"I don't know where Kit and Jenny went," Maggie said. "Can't you see I'm busy?"

"Where do you intend to send all those letters?" Duck demanded. "We don't know where John MacDonald went. He might be in California by now."

Maggie looked up at Duck with a ferocious glare. "Go away and leave me alone."

Duck sighed. *Maybe she'll never be normal again.* Finally she went to Uncle Levi. "Have you seen Jenny and Kit?" she asked.

Uncle Levi sat on a box nearby rubbing his sore feet. "Somebody's got to have seen them," Uncle Levi said and winked. "They can't have vanished into thin air."

Duck did not think he was being very funny. "Do you remember when you saw them last?" she asked.

Uncle Levi scratched his beard. "They were

walking ahead of the wagon train. Jenny told me she'd enjoy the trip more if she wasn't eating dust." He chuckled. "To enjoy such a trip along with such a crowd, a man must be able to endure heat like a salamander, mud and water like a muskrat, dust like a toad, and labor like a jackass. He must learn to sleep on the ground when it rains, share his blanket with vermin, and have patience with mosquitoes, who don't know any difference between the face of a man and the face of a mule. He must cease to think, except as to where he may find grass and water and a good camping place. It is a hardship without glory, to be sick without a home, to die and be buried like a dog."

Somehow Uncle Levi's fine speech backfired. Duck thought of poor little Wilkie and Mother, sick without a home, dead and buried. Maggie, who had been listening, burst into tears. Harvey turned away in disgust. "I'd beat some sense into him if he weren't my uncle," he muttered.

Uncle Levi cleared his throat uncomfortably. "Well, what do we do now?" he asked Duck in a helpless voice.

"I'll try to talk to Father," Duck said. She wandered over to the place where Father sat, staring into the fire. He was carving a sharp stick. Almost nothing was left. "Father?" she said softly. "We can't find Jenny. We can't find Kit. It's getting dark. What should we do, Father?"

For several moments he did not answer. He simply kept carving and staring.

"Father?" Duck asked again. "What should we do?"

"Nothing," he said finally. He threw the stick into the fire and watched it sizzle. He straightened up and stood, coming to his full height of six feet three inches.

Duck felt very, very small.

"We do nothing," he continued. "A night in the woods may do them good. They'll come back when it's light. They'll never wander off again like that, you can be sure."

"But, Father —"

"But nothing. I forbid you to do anything. Do you hear?"

Duck nodded slowly, but she was listening to other words. *Leaving you behind would teach you a lesson.* And a voice filled with bitterness along the Sweetwater. *Do you know what it is like to have six daughters?* Now Duck understood. If

Sonny and Harvey were lost, Father would go after them himself. But since two daughters were missing, what difference did it make?

Duck grit her teeth and walked away. At that moment she decided she was no longer her father's daughter. She *was* different. She would openly refuse to obey him. She would not sit idly by while Jenny and Kit were lost in the woods. Even if Jenny was sometimes proud and cruel and Kit could be vain and selfish. They were still her sisters. She had to help them — no matter how difficult it might be. *Doing what is right, no matter how hard.* Wasn't that what Uncle Levi had said?

"What'd Father say?" Fanny asked when she saw her putting a bridle on Shuttleback.

Duck told her.

"He's sick from grief. He doesn't know what he's saying," Fanny said. "But you better do what he says all the same."

"I don't care what he says," Duck replied. "I'm going." She ignored her oldest sister's warning. She swung on to the horse's bare back and rode west along the wagon road.

The forest that enclosed her was as black as the inside of a pocket. The trees stood close and thick. It took several minutes for Duck to get used to the lack of light. Kit was scared of the dark. Duck knew she had to hurry. Her sisters had undoubtedly wandered far ahead of the wagon train to get out of the dust. Where were they now? Perhaps they were close—maybe just around the next bend. But Duck did not see her sisters. She rode on and on. She called, hoping they hadn't left the wagon track. How could they see where they were going? It would be so easy to get lost. And what about the animals in the woods? Jenny was terrified of wolves. And what about Critchfield? What if he were still following them, angry with some kind of red-hot vengeance?

Something crashed through nearby trees. Shuttleback shied and plunged. A bear? Duck regained her balance and didn't need to prod Shuttleback faster. The horse broke into a trot. The sun had dropped behind the trees long ago. Strange noises echoed through the branches above. An owl hooted. Duck took up Grandfather's barred owl call to give herself courage. "Who-cooks-for-you!" she whistled. "Who-cooks-for-you-all?"

She rounded another bend. Where were her

sisters? Shuttleback hurried over slippery pine
needles, plunged, and kept moving. "Jenny?
Kit?" she called. "Where are you?"

Just as she was about to give up, she heard
the sound of voices. Someone ahead was crying.
She shouted her sisters' names again.

"We're here!" Jenny cried.

Duck followed her voice and found them
huddled on a fallen tree. The girls were over-
joyed. "You found us!" Jenny said.

Kit blew her nose on her apron. "We've been
waiting for hours and hours."

Jenny rubbed her feet. "We can't go on," she
said. "It's too cold. Oh, my shoe! My shoe!
However can I get along?"

"We've got to get back," Duck replied. Looking at them at that moment, she wondered if
they could have lasted all night. She decided not
to tell them that Father had forbidden her coming to find them. "You'll have to follow me. We
can make it. Come on, Jenny. Get up."

"I can't go on," Kit said dramatically. "I'll
collapse."

Duck sighed. "We'll take turns riding
Shuttleback."

Kit climbed atop the big horse. Shuttleback,

Jenny, and Duck picked their way uneasily over the slippery pine needles and fallen branches.

"That hurts!" Jenny complained, moving a limb out of the way.

"Whatever were you two doing?" Duck asked. "How did you get so far ahead?"

"Another train was just ahead of us," Jenny explained. "And Kit and myself wishing to—"

"Get out of the dust," interrupted Kit, "we decided to go ahead of the other wagon train. We walked and walked all afternoon."

"We thought that our teams would come up and meet us," Jenny said. "We thought you were all coming on up the road. So we went on and on and we finally came to an encampment."

"Some very pleasant people gave us a ride," Kit said. "The roads were good. Then they told us that you had all encamped two miles back."

"By that time it was sundown. It's so dark in these woods," Jenny said tearfully. "We started back anyway. Thank goodness you found us."

Duck listened to their story and didn't say anything. She was too busy watching the trees ahead. She had the feeling that bright eyes were following them. Somebody was watching. If she told her timid sisters, they'd become hysterical. Suddenly Shuttleback whinnied. The horse sensed someone, too.

"What's wrong?" Jenny whispered.

"Somebody's up ahead," Duck said in a low voice.

"An Indian?" Kit whined.

"What if it's a murderer?" Jenny whispered.

"Who are you?" Duck shouted as bravely as she could.

No answer.

"I think," Duck said in a loud voice, "that we should move along a little faster." She broke into a run, leading Shuttleback by the reins. Jenny ran with her. Kit leaned forward on the horse and held on for dear life.

"Is someone chasing us?" Jenny asked breathlessly.

"Maybe," said Duck.

"Ohhhh!" howled Kit. "We'll be killed."

"Shut up!" Duck shouted at her sister. She ran faster. Shuttleback wheezed.

"My feet hurt. I can't move much faster than this," Jenny shrieked. She tripped and fell and got up and kept running.

The faster they ran, the more frightened

Duck felt. Maybe there really was someone out there, maybe . . .

"You needn't pierce a poor man's skull with your caterwauling," a low voice said.

Kit screamed. The stranger stepped from the shadows and stood right in the middle of the road. The horse reared. Jenny dashed out of the way. Duck held on to the reins as tightly as she could to keep the horse from bolting into the trees and knocking off Kit.

"Who are you?" Duck demanded.

"I don't need to tell you my identity," the figure said and laughed. "Let's just say I'm a traveler."

"Wh-what do you want?" Kit stammered.

The stranger laughed unpleasantly.

Duck looked him over as best she could. All she could make out was a faint outline of nose and a shawl over his head. *He isn't a ghost, though,* she decided. Ghosts didn't smell like onions.

"You must have come past a wagon train beside the road. A little over a dozen people. Four wagons with oxen teams. Did you see them? How far away are we?"

The stranger chuckled. "Far."

"How far?"

"Far enough that no one there will hear you scream," the man said.

Kit began crying. "Leave us alone."

"Our father has a gun. He will hunt you down and he will kill you," Jenny said as bravely as she could.

"I don't care about your father. I'd like to know about your horse. Where did you find such a big, strong animal?" the man asked. There was something odd about him, Duck could tell. She could not make out his face, but she could see the outline of something large on his back. He looked as if he were carrying something heavy. "I could use a horse like that," he said and chuckled.

"This horse is not for sale," Duck said. "It's an old mean horse. She doesn't see too well. She's ugly. She bucks and she bites. You wouldn't want her."

"I'll let you pass if you give me the horse," the man said.

Duck wondered if the man had a gun or a knife. There were plenty of dangerous people on the road. Uncle Levi had told her of robbers that killed miners coming back from California.

If she gave the man the horse, would he spare their lives?

"This horse has no saddle," Duck said.

"I don't need a saddle," the man said. He reached up and took the reins from Duck. Shuttleback shied backward.

"Come down quickly," she hissed at Kit. In an instant Kit was on the ground, shivering beside Duck.

"Are you all sisters?" he asked.

"Y-y-yes we are," Jenny stammered.

"It would be a pity for your father to lose so many beautiful daughters," he said.

Kit started to cry again. "Take the horse," Duck said, "if that's what you want. Now go. We'll walk."

"Why, thank you!" the man said in a polite, mocking manner. "Don't mind if I do." He grunted and swung his pack up on to the horse. Then he pulled himself up onto the horse. Shuttleback sidestepped uneasily. The man pulled up hard on the reins. "It's going to be a long, long walk ahead for you."

"How far?" Kit asked fearfully.

"Five, seven miles, maybe more, through the darkest road I ever saw in my life," he said.

"I'm glad I'm on this horse. Fleet of foot is always best in a woods like this that's full of thieves and beggars."

"More thieves?" Jenny said, her voice squeaking.

"They're not such bad fellows," the man replied, laughing. "They're like me. They take from those that has and gives to those that hasn't. Well, I have places to go, things to see. Farewell. I'd take my hat off if I were a gentleman. But I'm not. Goodbye."

Duck reached out and held Shuttleback's halter with one hand. With the other she tenderly patted the horse. "Goodbye, Shuttleback," she whispered.

Chapter 14

The stranger turned Shuttleback and headed up the way the girls had just come. Duck listened to the horse's hooves pounding. "He's gone," Kit said with a sigh of relief.

"And he took our last horse," Duck replied sadly. "What will Father say?"

"I don't think we'll live long enough to worry about what Father thinks," Jenny said in a mournful voice. "The woods are full of more robbers—probably worse than that one."

"Then we'll run fast," Duck said. "Come on. They'll never catch us."

"I can't run seven miles," Kit complained.

Duck grabbed her by the arm. "Yes, you can. Run!"

The three girls ran and ran as fast as they could. To their amazement, it wasn't very long before they turned the bend and saw the light of their own campfire in a small clearing. Duck heard singing. Chat! They were back and they were safe. They slowed to a breathless stop.

"That stranger lied to us," Kit said angrily.

"He tricked us," Jenny agreed. "He told us it was miles and miles ahead."

"So we'd be quiet and let him take the horse," Duck said. She wondered what she would tell Father.

"Hallo!" shouted Harvey. "Who goes there?"

"Duck? Kit? Jenny?" Father called.

"You're all right!" Maggie shouted. She rushed to meet them. She planted an enormous kiss on the top of Duck's head.

Duck felt pleased and confused. *She missed me. Maybe she still likes me after all.*

Even more amazing was their greeting from Father. He gathered the three missing girls in his arms and gave them an enormous hug.

Duck felt breathless. She couldn't speak. Father never hugged anybody. She had never seen her father display such warm emotions toward her or any of her other brothers and sisters. "You were worried?" Duck asked, amazed. She had expected punishment, not this kind of welcome.

"Father was pacing a furrow three feet deep in the dirt," Harvey said. "Back and forth. Back and forth. 'Where can they be?' he kept saying over and over. 'Where are they?'"

Duck looked at Father. She saw him awkwardly wipe his eyes with his sleeve. "Duck," he said, "I'm glad you did what you thought was right."

"Father," she said quietly. "I have to tell you something. A robber on the road took Shuttleback. Our last horse."

"Shuttleback? He may find her more than he bargained for," Father said. "The main thing is that you're safe. We'll stay armed and on the lookout on the road ahead."

Duck smiled. Perhaps she and her sisters were more valuable to him than she had realized.

"Girls!" shouted Uncle Levi, joining the group after a breathless run across camp. "What happened?"

Duck told the whole story about how Jenny

and Kit were lost and how they met up with a thief.

"Well, you've returned in one piece. That's what matters. An adventure. What did I tell you, dearest Duck?" Uncle Levi said and winked. "This is reason to celebrate. Did you tell them, Harvey?"

"We have butter!" Harvey said gleefully.

"Real butter," Maggie added. "Two pounds. Father bought it from a peddler."

"He paid five whole dollars. Far, far too much," Fanny said. She displayed a serious expression, then grinned and tousled Duck's hair. "But I suppose you're worth it. Come eat." She led them to the campfire.

"Now that we've arrived in Oregon Territory," Harvey explained, "we're having a butter party to celebrate. Can you believe it? Butter. We haven't seen butter in months."

"Have a taste," said Chat.

"Eat hearty," added Sonny.

"Did the peddler smell like onions?" Duck demanded. Cautiously she scooped a bit of butter on the end of her finger and popped it into her mouth.

"Yes, and all other good things to eat," said

Fanny. "He carried flour and eggs and vegetables over from the other side of the pass. What an enterprising fellow! He'll make a bundle selling fresh food to hungry folks. He can charge whatever he wants."

Duck glanced at Jenny and Kit. Did they realize who the peddler was, too? She tried to decide whether to tell everyone that the man selling butter had taken not only Father's five dollars, but his last horse as well.

"With a bottle of oh-be-joyful, life would be perfect right now," said Uncle Levi dreamily. "But as it is, butter will have to do. Ten days on half allowance and two weeks without anything to eat! Lawd, Lawd the prospect tickles me!"

Duck took another quick swipe of the soft yellow butter. She would wait to tell about the peddler until *after* they finished enjoying the butter. She didn't want to spoil the party. How wonderful the butter tasted while it lasted!

She looked around the campfire at Uncle Levi and her five sisters and two brothers. They seemed so happy and carefree—joking and laughing. Even Father appeared relaxed, as if nothing terrible had ever happened to any of them. At that moment life appeared to be full of surprises. Amazing. Maybe Maggie had been right. Maybe everything would work out fine after all.

Something whinnied beyond the trees. There was a clatter of hoofbeats. "Why, look. It's Old Crowbait!" Harvey shouted.

"Shuttleback's returned!" Duck exclaimed. She jumped to her feet and ran to the old horse.

Uncle Levi chuckled. "Didn't you warn the thief how well that horse can throw a rider?"

Duck put her arm around the horse's neck. "I knew you'd find a way to come back," she whispered so that only Shuttleback could hear. She wiped the lather from the exhausted horse with a burlap sack. Then she led Shuttleback to a patch of grass and watched the hungry, tired horse graze.

When she returned to the fire, she noticed that Jenny was scribbling in her journal. Her sister sat in front of the dancing flames, deep in thought, wiggling her sore toes as she wrote.

"What are you writing?" Duck demanded. She took a seat beside her.

"About you. How you saved me and Kit," Jenny replied. "Read it so everybody can hear."

Duck took the journal. She cleared her throat and read aloud, " 'My sister, Kit, and myself wishing to get out of the dust, went ahead of it and walked all the afternoon, thinking our teams were coming on; we went within one mile of the next wagon train's encampment when we came to good roads and stopped to ride in the wagons when they should overtake us, where we were told that our wagons had encamped two miles back; it was the sun-down and the road back to our camp was through heavy timber, which appears dark in day light; we started back and met our brave little sister coming after us on horseback. She rode and found us and led us the long way back. . . .' "

"I wrote more," Jenny said and took the journal. She read aloud, " 'Then we met Father who was more uneasy if possible than we . . .' "

Duck looked at Father. He smiled. "I think that's an accurate portrait," he said softly.

Maggie gave Duck a proud hug. "You're a real heroine."

"A most truly remarkable young lady," Uncle Levi said.

"That's me," Duck said and grinned. "Dashing and brave, tall and free."

Afterword

This book is based on the adventures of a real family who made the trip west to Oregon Territory in 1852.

All six of the Scott sisters became suffrage movement supporters in Oregon when they grew up. Fanny became a Prohibition supporter, married a farmer, and lived to be ninety-seven — outliving all her family. Jenny, known as Abigail Scott Duniway, became a well-known novelist, newspaperwoman, speaker, and suffrage supporter. Mag and Kit worked on Harvey's newspaper, *The Oregonian,* a well-known Portland newspaper. Harvey was the only surviving

Scott brother after 1862, when Sonny died of tuberculosis. Chat became a musician and married a sheriff. And Duck became a spiritualist and medium. She married a carpenter and inventor and died in Seattle in 1930 at the age of eighty-nine, after publishing her own memoirs about the journey.

Bibliography

PRIMARY SOURCES

Duniway, Abigail Scott. "Narrative," in Scott, Harvey W., *History of the Oregon Country,* Vol. III. Cambridge: Riverside Press, 1924.

Duniway, Abigail Scott. *Path Breaking.* New York: Schocken Books, Inc., 1971. (autobiography)

Holmes, Kenneth L., editor. *Covered Wagon Women: Diaries and Letters from the Western Trails 1840–1890,* Vol. V. "Journal of a Trip to Oregon" by Abigail Jane Scott and "Scott Letters to Illinois and a Poem." Spokane, Washington: The Arthur H. Clark Co., 1986.

Marcy, Randolph B. *The Prairie Traveler: A Handbook for Overland Expeditions with Maps, Illus-*

trations and Itineraries of the Principal Routes Between the Mississippi and Pacific, published by the authority of the War Department, New York: Harper and Brothers, 1859. Reprint. Cambridge: Applewood Books, 1988.

Palmer, Harriet Scott. *Crossing Over the Great Plains by Ox-Wagons*, 1931. Printed privately.

PERIODICALS

Coburn, Catherine Scott. "Old Pioneer Days," *The Morning Oregonian*, June 20, 1890.

SOURCES

Federal Writers Project, *The Oregon Trail*, American Guide Series. New York: Hastings House, 1939.

McFarland, Gerald W. *A Scattered People: An American Family Moves West*. Amherst: University of Massachusetts Press, 1991.

Morrison, Dorothy Nafus. *Ladies Were Not Expected: Abigail Scott Duniway and Women's Rights*. New York: Atheneum, 1977.

Unruh, John D. Jr. *The Plains Across: The Overland Emigrants and the Trans-Mississippi West, 1840-60*. Chicago: University of Illinois Press, 1979.

Werner, Emmy E. *Pioneer Children on the Journey West.* Boulder: Westview Press, A Division of HarperCollins Publishers, Inc., 1995.

West, Elliott. *Growing Up with the Country: Childhood on the Far Western Frontier.* Albuquerque: University of New Mexico Press, 1989.

About the Author

Trained as a journalist, Laurie Lawlor worked for many years as a freelance writer and editor before devoting herself full-time to the creation of children's books. She enjoys many speaking engagements at schools and libraries, and her books have been nominated for many awards. She lives in Evanston, Illinois, with her husband, son, daughter, and two large Labrador retrievers. Her books include the *Addie Across the Prairie* series, the *Heartland* series, *How to Survive Third Grade*, *The Worm Club*, *Gold in the Hills*, and *Little Women* (a movie novelization). Her nonfiction work, *Shadow Catcher: The Life and Work of Edward S. Curtis*, won the Carl Sandburg Award for nonfiction (1995) and the Golden Kite Honor Book Award (1995).